D0291786

TIME FOR A REAL ADVENTURE

Something caught Stevie's eye over Phil's shoulder. On a sale table near the cash register was a display of trip journals—little red plaid books of blank pages to write on. "Hey!" she cried. "I've got a great idea! Let's each get one of these and keep a diary of our trip. Then, when we get back home, we can share them with each other. It'll be like writing one long letter full of all the interesting stuff we might forget."

"That is a great idea." Phil turned around and grabbed two journals off the shelf. He handed one to her. "One for you and one for me. That way I'll learn all about the Oregon Trail and you'll learn all about white-water rafting. It's almost like going on two vacations."

"Well, almost, but not quite." Stevie laughed. "Look, I've got to go. I hope you have a wonderful trip, Phil."

Phil gave her a gentle smile. "Same here, Stevie. I'll call you as soon as I get back to town." He waved to Lisa and Carole. "Have a great vacation! I'm sure the Oregon Trail will never be the same!"

Other Skylark Books you will enjoy
Ask your bookseller for the books you have missed

THE WINNING STROKE (American Gold Swimmers #1)
by Sharon Dennis Wyeth

COMPETITION FEVER (American Gold Gymnasts #1)
by Gabrielle Charbonnet

THE GREAT DAD DISASTER *by Betsy Haynes*

THE GREAT MOM SWAP *by Betsy Haynes*

BREAKING THE ICE (Silver Blades #1) *by Melissa Lowell*

SAVE THE UNICORNS (Unicorn Club #1) *by Francine Pascal*

THE SADDLE CLUB

WAGON TRAIL

BONNIE BRYANT

A SKYLARK BOOK
NEW YORK • TORONTO • LONDON • SYDNEY • AUCKLAND

RL 5, 009–012

WAGON TRAIL

A Bantam Skylark Book / August 1998

Skylark Books is a registered trademark of Bantam Books, a division
of Bantam Doubleday Dell Publishing Group, Inc. Registered in U.S. Patent
and Trademark Office and elsewhere.

"The Saddle Club" is a registered trademark of Bonnie Bryant Hiller.
The Saddle Club design/logo, which consists of a riding crop
and a riding hat, is a trademark of Bantam Books.

"USPC" and "Pony Club" are registered trademarks of The United States
Pony Clubs, Inc., at The Kentucky Horse Park, 4071 Iron Works Pike,
Lexington, KY 40511-8462.

All rights reserved.
Copyright © 1998 by Bonnie Bryant Hiller.
Cover art © 1998 by Paul Casale.
No part of this book may be reproduced or transmitted in any form or
by any means, electronic or mechanical, including photocopying, recording,
or by any information storage and retrieval system, without permission in
writing from the publisher.
For information address: Bantam Books.

If you purchased this book without a cover you should be aware that this book
is stolen property. It was reported as "unsold and destroyed" to the publisher,
and neither the author nor the publisher has received any payment for this
"stripped book."

ISBN 0-553-48631-4

Published simultaneously in the United States and Canada.

Bantam Books are published by Bantam Books, a division of Bantam Doubleday Dell
Publishing Group, Inc. Its trademark, consisting of the words "Bantam Books" and
the portrayal of a rooster, is Registered in U.S. Patent and Trademark Office and in
other countries. Marca Registrada. Bantam Books, 1540 Broadway, New York, New
York 10036.

PRINTED IN THE UNITED STATES OF AMERICA

OPM   0 9 8 7 6 5 4 3 2 1

*I would like to express my special thanks
to Sallie Bissell for her help
in the writing of this book.*

*Thanks also to Ellen Levine,
who helped me find the trail.*
—B.B.

RECEIVED SEP 0 4 1998

THOROLD PUBLIC LIBRARY

"Whew!" Stevie Lake unbuckled her riding helmet and wiped the sweat from her forehead. "I don't think I've ever gone over so many cavalletti in one hour. I was beginning to feel like a Mexican jumping bean."

Carole Hanson smiled as she clipped her horse, Starlight, to a set of cross-ties. "I know what you mean, Stevie. But just think. If you feel like a Mexican jumping bean, then these horses must feel like kangaroos!"

"I vote that we rub them down and then cool ourselves off over at TD's with an ice cream," suggested Lisa Atwood, running a dandy brush over Prancer's damp withers.

"That's a great idea!" Stevie said. "I'm amazed I didn't think of it first."

"Actually, Stevie, we're amazed you didn't think of it first, too," Carole laughed.

The girls continued to groom their horses. Stevie loosened Belle's leg wraps while Carole and Lisa gave Starlight and Prancer a good brushing.

"You know, it's too bad Max doesn't have one of those electronic horse groomers," Stevie said as she brushed Belle's thick mane.

"An electronic horse groomer?" Lisa frowned.

"Yeah. Remember that thing Judy used on Danny? It looked like a little vacuum cleaner," explained Stevie.

"Oh, right," said Carole. "But I can't help wondering how the horse feels about being treated like a piece of carpet."

"I don't know," Stevie said, chuckling. "But Judy loved it! And Danny didn't seem to mind."

"There you three are!" A woman's excited voice rang out from the far end of the stable.

The girls turned. Deborah Hale, Max Regnery's wife, hurried toward them, their baby girl, Maxi, in her arms. "Max said you had just finished the advanced jumps class and were probably on your way to TD's. I'm so glad I caught you!"

"What's up, Deborah?" Lisa shot a puzzled glance at Stevie and Carole.

2

Deborah spoke in a rush. "I just got a call from Bart Charles, an editor down at the paper. He wants me to write a feature article, but first I need to go into the city to meet with him this afternoon. I can't take Maxi with me, and Max has three private lessons this afternoon, so I was wondering if you girls could help me out and sit with Maxi." She looked at The Saddle Club pleadingly.

"Sure." Carole answered for all of them without hesitation. "We'd be glad to."

"After all, that's what The Saddle Club is for—to help each other out whenever we need it." Stevie grinned. "And, Deborah, you and Maxi and Max are all honorary Saddle Club members."

"Wonderful," Deborah said with relief. "I'll go home and get ready. You guys come on over when you finish with your horses. Maxi and I will be waiting." Smiling happily, she hurried with Maxi out of the cool, dark stable and into the bright summer day.

After the girls finished grooming their horses, they put them back in their stalls with an extra armload of hay and walked over to the white clapboard farmhouse where Max and Deborah lived. It was up a slight hill just behind the stable. Deborah and Maxi were sitting in the wide porch swing, waiting for them.

"I can't tell you how much I appreciate this." Deborah smiled. She'd changed out of her jeans and was wearing a blue business suit that matched her eyes.

"It'll be fun," said Lisa.

"Well, just remember, Maxi's crawling now, and anything she can pick up goes immediately into her mouth. She ought to be ready for her nap in a little while, so this should be pretty easy baby-sitting. If you have any problems, though, just run down to the stable. Max and Mrs. Reg are both there and can help in an emergency." Deborah handed Maxi to Carole and checked her watch. "I've got to go! Thanks so much, girls. I'll see you in a couple of hours."

"Good luck!" Stevie called as Deborah ran to her car. "Don't worry about a thing."

"Ouch, Maxi! Let go!" Carole yelped. Maxi had grabbed one of Carole's small stirrup-shaped earrings and was trying to put it into her mouth. "I need that ear for the rest of summer vacation!"

"Come to Aunt Stevie, Maxi." Stevie held out her arms and tried to distract the baby from Carole's ear. Maxi gurgled, let go of the earring, and allowed Stevie to take her. Stevie began walking her up and down the porch, but stopped when Maxi grabbed a fistful of her long honey blond hair.

"Ow, Maxi!" Stevie cried. "That hair was attached to my head!" Maxi giggled and pulled even harder.

"Why don't we put her in her playpen?" Lisa suggested. "Deborah said it was almost time for her nap."

4

"Good idea," said Stevie, wincing with pain as Maxi yanked another handful of hair. "Otherwise I might wind up bald."

Lisa held the door open while Stevie carried Maxi into the house. Her playpen was set up in the living room. After Carole cleared it of a stuffed Big Bird and a plastic ball, Stevie laid Maxi down on her stomach. Immediately the baby rolled over and sat up, but Stevie and Lisa and Carole had already begun to tiptoe toward the kitchen.

"It's time for you to take a nap now, Maxi," Carole whispered as Maxi blinked. "Don't worry. We'll be right in here."

The girls gently closed the door and sat down at the kitchen table.

"How can we tell what's she doing in there if we're sitting in here?" Stevie frowned with concern.

"Haven't you ever seen one of these?" Lisa switched on a white plastic box that looked like a small radio.

"No," replied Stevie. "I don't baby-sit all that much. My last job was feeding Mrs. Perkins's parakeets."

Lisa smiled. "Well, this is even better than an electronic horse groomer. This is a baby monitor." She turned the dial. "Listen."

The girls bent over and listened to the monitor. They heard a slight rustling noise.

"Sounds like she might be getting comfortable to go to sleep," said Carole. "I wish my CD player sounded that clear."

"I wish my CD-ROM sounded like anything at all," complained Stevie. "I was up to the final level of that game Squelch when stupid Chad crashed the hard drive. Now the only thing the computer can say is 'You have performed an illegal operation. . . .' "

"Shhh!" Lisa said suddenly. "Listen."

The girls leaned over the monitor again. The gentle rustling noise had stopped. They heard a little chirp, then a louder whimper, and then a full-fledged cry.

"Come on," Lisa said as she got up from her chair. "Let's go calm·her down and maybe we can get her to go to sleep."

The girls trooped back into the living room. Maxi was sitting up in her playpen, huge tears rolling down her cheeks. She lifted her arms to be picked up.

"Poor baby Maxi," Lisa said as she scooped up the child. "Let's put you in your chair swing and see if that makes you sleepy."

Lisa buckled Maxi into her swing while Stevie wound the motor.

"You know about chair swings, Stevie?" Carole asked with a laugh.

"Sure I do," replied Stevie. "My mom just sold my old one at a garage sale."

6

The girls sat and watched as the swing rocked Maxi back and forth. Slowly her eyelids began to droop, but then, as soon as she realized she was falling asleep, she jerked her head up and began to cry all over again.

"I don't think the swing is working," said Stevie as Maxi's sobs grew louder.

"Maybe some music would help," Carole suggested. She jumped up and began thumbing through some CDs that were stacked on a bookcase. She pulled one from the pile. "Here's a good one. *Beethoven, Bach, and the Glorious Sounds of Nature.*"

Carole put the CD into the player and turned up the volume. Suddenly the room was filled with a pipe organ blaring through the sounds of a summer storm. Maxi jumped straight up at the first clap of thunder and then started yowling more loudly than ever.

"Cut the music!" Lisa said, wide-eyed. "It's scaring her to death!" She unbuckled Maxi from the chair swing and held her in her arms. Maxi's face was red with rage, and she was hiccuping as well as crying. Lisa frowned at Stevie and Carole. "Don't just stand there! Think of something we can do to calm her down!"

"I know!" Stevie cried. "Let's show her a video!" She knelt down in front of the TV and rummaged through a stack of videotapes. "Here's one!" she said. "Cartoons. That should work fine."

Stevie slid the tape into the VCR, and with Lisa

holding Maxi, they all huddled in front of the TV to watch. Maxi quit crying as a pink elephant waltzed across the screen, but instead of growing sleepy, she started laughing and clapping her hands.

After a few minutes of the elephant's dance, Stevie looked over at Maxi. The baby's eyes were clear and bright. "This tape is great for cheering her up," she said, "but it sure isn't helping to put her to sleep."

They were watching another video when the front door opened. Deborah appeared in the living room, little wisps of red hair escaping from the bun at the base of her neck. "Hi, everybody," she called. "How's it going?"

The Saddle Club and Maxi rose from in front of the TV.

"Deborah!" Stevie said as Maxi held out her arms to her mother. "We're so glad you're back."

Deborah laughed and grinned at Maxi. "Are you having too much fun to take a nap, sugar?" she asked. She held Maxi close for a moment and smiled at her frazzled-looking baby-sitters. "Why don't you girls get something to eat? There's pizza in the freezer. Nuke it in the microwave while I take Maxi to her room and see if I can get her to sleep."

Deborah whirled Maxi down the hall while The Saddle Club retreated to the kitchen. By the time they had microwaved the pizza, Deborah had returned. "There," she said as she switched the baby monitor from the living room to Maxi's room. "She's sleeping like the proverbial baby."

"You're kidding." Stevie almost dropped the slice of pizza that was halfway to her mouth.

"No." Deborah smiled. "She seemed glad to get into her little crib."

"We tried to get her to sleep," Lisa explained as Deborah opened a big bottle of soda for everyone, "but nothing seemed to help."

"Right," said Carole. "We tried the baby swing, the Beethoven CD, and finally cartoons. We were about to run out of stuff to try."

"Since they've got electronic horse groomers, what they need to invent now is an electronic baby soother," Stevie said. "Life is tough enough without having to deal with all that crying."

Deborah shook her head and chuckled.

"What so funny?" cried Stevie. "I think a baby-soothing machine is a great idea!"

"Oh, it is, Stevie." Deborah nodded. "It just reminded me of the meeting I was in."

"Oh?" said Carole. "What was your meeting about?"

"About doing an article on the pioneers who crossed the prairies in covered wagons. If you think things are tough without a baby-soothing machine, you should have seen what traveling with a baby was like over a hundred years ago."

"That's true, but what's the big deal?" said Stevie. "I mean, that's the way people had to live back then. Today we've got computers and microwaves and televisions."

Deborah took some pizza for herself. "Actually, we still do have covered wagons today. I just met with the travel editor of my paper. He wants me to fly out West and go on a wagon train reenactment, then write an article about it."

"Neat," said Carole.

Deborah chewed her pizza thoughtfully. "Somebody recommended me, because they figured Max Regnery's wife must know a lot about horses. On the way home I decided that I should probably turn this assignment down, because my background isn't in horses, but maybe I was too hasty. After all, it's not important for me to be savvy about animals and the environment, as long as I'm with someone who is."

"Yes," Lisa said. "Max knows a lot about animals."

Deborah grinned at the girls. "Actually, I wasn't thinking about Max. He can't take time away from the stable right now. I was thinking about you guys. How would The Saddle Club like to go West? You know all about horses. It's a weeklong trip, and the newspaper will pay for a family of four. Maxi's too young to go, but I've got plenty of time to line up a baby-sitter. Sound like anything you'd be interested in?"

"Oh, boy!" cried Stevie. "Would we ever!"

"Count me in," Carole added with a grin. "I'd love to see if I'm as tough as the old trailblazers."

"I'd love to go, too," said Lisa. "But the toughest trail I'll have to blaze will be convincing my mother to let me be a modern-day pioneer."

"This should be it!" Stevie cried as she lunged across her bed to answer the phone for the fifteenth time that night. After The Saddle Club had left Deborah and Maxi, each girl had scurried home to ask her parents' permission to go on the wagon train reenactment. There had been flurries of phone calls among Deborah, the Hansons, the Atwoods, and the Lakes. Slowly, the details were explained and the permissions were granted. Carole could go. Stevie could go. But they were still waiting to hear from the last holdout, Mrs. Atwood.

"Oh, please say she said yes," Stevie said into the phone without bothering to say hello.

"She said yes!" Lisa's voice came through the receiver. "It took some real convincing, but she finally said okay."

"All right!" cried Stevie. "Now The Saddle Club can go on the Oregon Trail!"

"Won't it be fun?" replied Lisa. "I can hardly wait. I've got so much to do I'd better get off the phone. It seems like I've been talking all night."

"I know what you mean." Stevie massaged her left ear. "I've got lots to do, too. I'll call you first thing tomorrow."

Stevie hung up the phone, tired of talking but glad that both her best friends were going out West with her. It would be their best vacation ever. She leaped off her bed. A trip down the Oregon Trail was something she could really gloat about in front of Chad. She had just opened her bedroom door to go find him when the phone rang again.

"Oh, please!" she said as she leaped onto the bed again. "Hello?" she answered hurriedly.

A husky, nonfemale voice came over the phone. "Hi, Stevie. This is Phil."

"Oh, hi, Phil," Stevie replied more softly. "How are you?"

"I'm good. What on earth is going on? Your line's been busy for hours."

"Oh, just some Saddle Club plans to work out."

THOROLD PUBLIC LIBRARY

Stevie twisted the telephone cord around her finger. "What's up with you?"

"Well, something great just happened. About a month ago my dad made reservations for the whole family to go on a white-water rafting trip down the Colorado River. We were all set to go until yesterday, when my sister got this summer job that she's been dying to have. Now she wants to stay here with friends and work while we go on our trip. That leaves one space that's been reserved and will have to be paid for. I was wondering if you'd like to come with us. My mom and dad said it would be okay."

"That sounds wonderful!" Visions of paddling through rapids of foamy white water flashed through Stevie's mind. "I'd love to! But I'll have to ask my parents."

"I know. Get a pencil and I'll give you all the details."

"Okay. Hang on." Stevie searched frantically around her room for a pencil, finally finding a short, stubby one under her bed. A wadded-up piece of notebook paper was under the bed as well, so she smoothed it out and used it to scribble down Phil's information.

"This sounds really neat, Phil. I'm so glad you invited me. As soon as I get some kind of semiofficial answer from my parents, I'll call you back."

"I sure hope they say yes, Stevie," Phil said.

"Oh, I do, too. I'll talk to you soon!"

Stevie hung up the phone and looked at the notes she'd scrawled on the paper. Something seemed vaguely familiar about the dates, but she couldn't quite place it. Finally it hit her. Phil was going rafting at exactly the same time she had just promised to go on the Oregon Trail!

"Oh no," she said, her fingers automatically dialing Carole's number. "This is terrible."

"You'll never guess what just happened," Stevie blurted out as soon as Carole answered the phone.

"Your parents took back their permission for the Oregon Trail because you did something awful to Chad." Carole had known Stevie to get in trouble like this on more than one occasion.

"No, nothing like that. Phil just called and invited me to go with his family on a white-water rafting trip on exactly the same dates as the wagon train."

"Oh no!" said Carole. "That's terrible. Are you positive the dates are the same?"

"Yes," Stevie replied miserably, studying her scribbled notes. "I'm looking at them right here in black and white. They fly out West on Monday, then start rafting on Tuesday. Just think, Carole, it would be rafting with Phil and camping along the way and having a great time!"

Carole sighed. "That's a tough call, Stevie. Phil's trip

sounds wonderful, but don't forget that you did promise to do the wagon train trip, and Deborah is counting on all three of us."

"I know," replied Stevie.

"Plus, the newspaper is paying for the Oregon Trail trip. Wouldn't your parents have to pay for your part of Phil's trip?"

"Yes, they would."

"Well, Stevie, there's your answer. No parent would pay for an expensive rafting trip when you have another equally fabulous trip waiting for you for free."

"I hadn't thought of it that way, but you're right." Stevie knew her parents were generous, but she also knew that money was always tight in a family of four children.

"Anyway," Carole continued, "who says it might not be a good thing for you and Phil to be apart for a while?"

"What do you mean?" asked Stevie.

"You know that old saying 'absence makes the heart grow fonder'? You'll have plenty to do on the wagon train trip, but if all Phil's doing is paddling down a river, he might begin to think about you a lot."

"Think so?" Stevie pictured Phil pulling a paddle through the Colorado River, all the while seeing her face on the sunlit boulders, in the foamy white water, in the blue sky above.

"Yes," said Carole. "He might come back a totally different person."

"Well, I don't know that I want him to be totally different, but a little different might be okay," Stevie said with a smile. "I think you're right, Carole. I think it would be crazy for me not to go on a totally free, totally neat trip. Plus it might be the best thing in the world for Phil and me. I'm going to call him back right now and tell him!"

Stevie hung up the phone and dialed Phil's number. His sister answered; then Phil came on the line.

"Hi, Phil, this is Stevie."

"Hi, Stevie. Did you ask your parents about the trip?"

"Well, no. Actually, after we hung up I realized that your trip is scheduled at exactly the same time as a trip I promised to go on with The Saddle Club."

"What kind of trip?"

"It's a wagon train reenactment along the Oregon Trail. Max's wife, Deborah, is writing an article about it for the paper, and since Max can't go and we know all about horses, the paper is paying our way to go along with her."

"Didn't you know about this trip when I called before?" Phil sounded annoyed.

"Yes, but I didn't realize the dates were the same. I'm sorry. I've talked to so many people on the phone tonight, I just got mixed up."

"That's too bad, Stevie. I was really looking forward to you coming along. Now my little sister will get to invite her best friend, Sarah Groom."

Stevie frowned. "So what's wrong with Sarah Groom? She's a neat little kid."

"Yeah. Well, she's a neat little kid who's got this weird crush on me. Every time I say anything to her she just turns red and starts sighing."

Stevie laughed. "Gee, Phil, it must be pretty tough to have all these younger women throwing themselves at you."

"Stevie, you know that's not what I mean," Phil said.

"I know. I was just teasing. I really wish I could go on this trip with you, but I promised Deborah that I would go with her first, and a promise is a promise." Stevie smiled and coiled the telephone cord around her finger again. "Anyway, it might be good for us to take separate vacations."

"What do you mean?" Phil sounded surprised.

"I mean, you know how sometimes when you're away from a person you really like, you can begin to see them differently and it makes you realize how much you like them all over again? In fact, it makes you like them even better?"

"Yeah, I suppose," Phil admitted.

"Well, just think. By the time we both get back from

our vacations, we'll really have missed each other and we'll like each other all the more!"

Phil sighed. "I guess you're right, Stevie. But I still wish you were coming with us instead of Sarah."

"I do, too, Phil. But think of how great it'll be when we finally get back together!"

On that they said good-bye; then Stevie immediately dialed Carole and Lisa on three-way calling.

"I solved my Phil problem," Stevie announced proudly.

"How?" Lisa asked. "Carole just called and told me that he had asked you to go rafting at the same time as our wagon train trip."

"Well, first I explained to him that I'd promised you guys and Deborah first and that I had just gotten confused on the dates."

"What did he say?" asked Carole.

"He was real disappointed, because that meant his little sister would get to invite her best friend, Sarah Groom, who has a big crush on Phil."

"Uh-oh," said Lisa.

"No, it's okay," Stevie assured her. "Phil thinks Sarah is a pest. And anyway, I convinced Phil that the best thing in the world for us would be to be apart for a few days. We can see new sights and meet new people, and when we get back home we'll appreciate each other all the more."

"Did he believe that?" Lisa asked.

"He seemed to," replied Stevie. "Anyway, *I* think it's a great idea. Just think of all the new people we'll meet. Why, maybe you and Carole will meet some terrific guys on the wagon train."

"We might, Stevie," Carole laughed, "but so might you!"

"Me?" Stevie asked incredulously. "I don't think so."

"You never know!" teased Lisa.

Stevie started to reply, but a thought stopped her cold. She didn't think it would be possible for her to meet anybody half as cute and funny as Phil, but it was entirely possible that Phil might meet somebody a whole lot cuter and funnier than she was. And not just Sarah Groom. Lots of different people went on those rafting trips. What if some really cute girl fell out of her raft? Phil would leap in the river and rescue her and then their eyes would meet and they would fall—

"Stevie, are you still there?" Lisa's voice crackled over the phone.

"Huh?" Stevie pushed the thought of Phil and the cute half-drowned girl to the back of her mind. "Yes, I'm still here."

"Can you go to the mall with Deborah and us tomorrow? We need to get some supplies for the trip."

"Sure. What time?"

"Deborah said Max could watch Maxi at noon. Let's meet at the stable at about eleven-thirty."

"Sounds good to me," said Carole. "I'll see you two there tomorrow."

"Bye, Carole; bye, Lisa. See you tomorrow," Stevie said. She hung up the phone and massaged her ear again. The vision of Phil and the cute girl popped back into her head, but she ignored it. "Travel broadens your horizons," she told herself resolutely. "And if Phil's horizons are getting broadened, then mine will just have to be, too."

"Which store do we want to do first?" Carole asked as she followed Deborah, Stevie, and Lisa into the mall. "I need a couple of pairs of socks."

"I could use some socks, too," said Stevie. She sniffed the air, then turned toward one corner of the mall, where the aroma of baking cookies rose from a small storefront café. "I could also use a large chocolate macadamia nut cookie."

"Let's get our shopping done first," Lisa said. "Then we can pig out on cookies."

"Did anybody bring a list?" asked Deborah.

Stevie and Carole shook their heads, but Lisa gave Deborah a resigned smile. "I did. Or at least my mother sent my packing list along. I don't need to buy that much on it." She reached in her purse for a sheet of paper. On it was a typed list of supplies Mrs. Atwood wanted Lisa to take.

"My mother is afraid that the nights will be cold. So she thinks I should take three sweaters, a down jacket, a heavy-duty sleeping bag with two extra blankets, two pillows, three sets of gloves, three sets of long underwear, moisturizing sunscreen, and a pair of earmuffs."

"Earmuffs?" Stevie frowned. "Where are you going to buy earmuffs in June?"

Lisa squinted at her list. "Actually, I already have earmuffs and most of the other things on this list. I just have to buy what my mother's typed an asterisk beside." She looked at her friends, then turned the page over and continued. "Then I have to get aspirin, bandages, cough syrup, decongestant, antihistamine, vitamins, and throat lozenges." She shrugged. "She thinks I might catch a cold."

"And I think you'll be suffering from exhaustion if you pack all that stuff," said Carole.

"Wait a minute." Deborah stopped in the middle of the mall. "Lisa, I know your mother wants to take good care of you, but I don't think she understands the nature of a wagon train reenactment. This is not going to be a cushy trip. We're really going to be traveling by covered wagon. We'll be responsible for all of our clothes and provisions ourselves. Unless you can fit all these things into a single backpack that you can carry, you're going to have to leave a lot of things along the trail."

Lisa blinked. "Along the trail?"

"Yes. It's going to be just like the old days, and the old days were awfully rough. People had to trash treasured items they brought from back East because they couldn't get them through the mud or over the mountains. It wasn't uncommon to see horsehair sofas and dining room tables and even pianos abandoned by the side of the trail."

"Wow," said Carole, her dark eyes wide with wonder.

Deborah went on. "We're going to have to travel light. I mean *really* light. Here's the list they faxed me." She unfolded a single sheet of paper. A short list of supplies covered the top half of the page, with the instructions in big capital letters: ALL YOUR SUPPLIES MUST FIT INTO ONE LARGE BAG.

"Gosh," Stevie said. "They aren't kidding. But why do we have to take laundry soap?"

Deborah laughed. "Because the directors of this trip want us to live as closely as possible to the lives the settlers lived. That means we'll be wearing pioneer clothing and washing both our clothes and ourselves in creeks along the way. No showers, no bathrooms, no hot water." She smiled at the girls' open mouths. "This

24

trip is to be as authentic as possible without endangering the participants."

"Cool," said Stevie.

"Sounds fun to me," agreed Carole.

"I'm all for it, too," said Lisa. "But we can't tell my mother. She'll never let me go if I don't take everything on this list with me."

The girls frowned for a moment, thinking. Then Stevie grinned. "I know what we can do. Let your mother pack all this stuff for you, and then you can bring it over to my house and stash it there during the trip. That way your mother'll think you've taken everything, and you can take only what you need."

"Would your mom mind?" Lisa asked.

Stevie shook her head. "We'll put your suitcases in my closet. My mom's afraid to go in my closet." She shrugged. "For that matter, everybody's afraid to go in my closet."

Carole laughed. "Why am I not surprised?"

Deborah raised one eyebrow at the giggling girls. "I know this sounds like a lot of fun to you guys now, but are you sure you can do without your computer games and your CDs and your VCRs for a whole week?"

"Sure we can," said Carole. "This is a real adventure instead of just goofy fake cyber-stuff."

"Okay." Deborah smiled. "Just wanted to be sure we were all on the same page here." She held up the short list of supplies again. "So who needs what from this list?"

The girls peered at the paper. "I've got all of that stuff at home," said Stevie. "Except the biodegradable soap."

"Me too," Lisa said.

"Me three," added Carole. "But I still need to buy some socks."

"Well, I think we can get the soap at the sporting goods store, which is down that way." Deborah pointed past the café. "I'm sure they have socks there, too."

They walked down to the sporting goods store, passing a computer software outlet and a music shop along the way.

Stevie gazed at a giant software display. "I wonder if they have the new version of Squelch."

"I don't know," replied Carole. "I was kind of wondering if the music store had the new Shimmery Emery CD." She stopped for an instant, then shook her head. "Stevie, what are we talking about? The day after tomorrow we're going to be living in a world without computers or CD players or anything."

Stevie grinned sheepishly. "I know, but we'll be back in a week. Should be a real challenge, huh?"

At the sporting goods store, Stevie and Carole found socks they liked, and everybody grabbed a big plastic bottle of liquid peppermint soap. They were standing in line to check out when Stevie heard a voice behind her.

"Hey, Stevie!"

She turned. Phil and his father stood there with a half-filled shopping cart.

"Hi, Phil. Hi, Mr. Marsten." She walked over to talk to them.

Phil's father smiled. "What are you doing here, Stevie? I figured you made most of your purchases at the tack shop."

"Oh, we had to get some biodegradable soap for our wagon train trip. We're going to be washing our clothes in creeks along the way."

Phil eyed the bottle Stevie held up. "Your trip sounds really neat, Stevie. You'll be like real pioneers."

"That's right." Stevie looked over at the Marstens' cart. It was filled with a cookstove, sleeping bags, and a cooler. "Looks like you're going to be taking a pretty neat trip yourself, Phil." She smiled at him. "I'm sorry it didn't work out that we could be together."

"I'm sorry, too. It would have been lots of fun."

Something caught Stevie's eye over Phil's shoulder. On a sale table near the cash register was a display of trip journals—little red plaid books of blank pages to write in. "Hey!" she cried. "I've got a great idea! Let's each get one of these and keep a diary of our trip. Then, when we get back home, we can share them with each other. It'll be like writing one long letter full of all the interesting stuff we might forget."

"That is a great idea." Phil turned around and grabbed two journals off the shelf. He handed one to her. "One for you and one for me. That way I'll learn all about the Oregon Trail and you'll learn all about white-water rafting. It's almost like going on two vacations."

"Well, almost, but not quite." Stevie laughed. "Look, I've got to go. I hope you have a wonderful trip, Phil."

Phil gave her a gentle smile. "Same here, Stevie. I'll call you as soon as I get back to town." He waved to Lisa and Carole. "Have a great vacation! I'm sure the Oregon Trail will never be the same!"

"Thanks, Phil," called Carole. "Hope you have a good vacation, too."

Stevie waved to Phil, then rejoined her friends at the checkout line. After they had paid for their supplies, they walked slowly toward the entrance of the mall. Again the scent of fresh-baked cookies wafted through the air.

"I have a suggestion," said Stevie.

"I bet it has something to do with those cookies," Lisa laughed.

"Well, kind of. Since we're leaving the day after tomorrow, and since tomorrow we'll be busy packing and taking our last horseback ride at Pine Hollow, I vote we each get a cookie and drink a toast to our last contact with the modern world."

"Stevie, you can't drink a toast with a cookie," Carole said.

"Yeah, but we can click our cookies together before we take our first bite. That'll be just as good as a toast."

"Actually, I think that's a terrific idea," said Deborah. "They certainly won't be delivering any warm chocolate macadamia nut cookies on the Oregon Trail!"

"There!" Stevie shoved Lisa's last suitcase into the back of her closet. "Safe and sound. Two suitcases all hidden away for your vacation."

"Are you sure your mother won't find these and call my mother?" Lisa's blue eyes clouded with worry as she stuffed the last of her supplies into a single duffel bag.

"Absolutely." Stevie pointed to her closet. "Would you willingly look for something in there if you didn't desperately need it?"

Carole and Lisa gazed at the jumbled array of books, shoes, clothes, papers, and old school projects that spilled from the closet.

"I think you're safe, Lisa." Carole's easy laugh was reassuring. "Even if Mrs. Lake were looking for your luggage, she probably couldn't find it for a couple of weeks, anyway."

"Hey, Stevie!" Stevie's brother Chad yelled from the living room. "Max and Deborah are here."

"All right!" Stevie grabbed her backpack. "Westward ho, pioneers!"

The girls said good-bye to the Lakes, then piled into the Pine Hollow van. "How's everybody doing this afternoon?" Max asked as he turned toward the airport. "Are you guys ready to rough it?"

"We sure are." Carole smoothed her long dark hair back behind her ears.

"And are you fully aware of how much you'll be expected to work during this trip?" Deborah asked from the front seat.

"Don't worry," answered Stevie. "We've worked real hard at the Devines' dude ranch. And we've had a lot of experience in riding Western."

Deborah frowned. "Well, don't forget you'll be riding Western in authentic costumes. Hats, bonnets, skirts."

"Skirts?" A note of alarm rose in Stevie's voice.

"Yes. Skirts. The whole nine historically correct yards."

"Will we have to ride sidesaddle?" Lisa asked.

"Good question," Deborah replied. "I don't know. I know we'll all be assigned roles to play, where we'll assume the lives of people who actually might have gone along the trail. That's done at Plimoth Plantation and a lot of other historic sites."

"Cool." Stevie fluttered her eyelashes. "Maybe they'll let me be somebody famous, like that opera singer, Jenny Lind."

Lisa shook her head. "Stevie, they'll be more likely to typecast you as Calamity Jane."

An hour later, they all said good-bye to Max and Maxi and boarded the plane that would take them out West. "This is so cool," Carole breathed as the plane gathered speed and hurtled down the runway. "If I weren't so crazy about horses, I'd be crazy about flying."

"Then we'd have to change the name of our club," said Lisa. "We'd have to be something like The Silver Wings Club instead of The Saddle Club."

"That might be neat," Stevie said, looking out the window as the landscape rushed by. "But I don't think it would be as much fun."

Just as the sun was disappearing behind the mountains, their plane landed in what looked like a wide patch of Western prairie. Deborah hailed one of the few taxis available at the small regional airport, and soon they were deposited in front of a rambling old hotel called the Wagon Train Lodge.

"Wow," Carole said as Deborah paid the cabdriver. "Let's go look at all the covered wagons parked by the corral!"

"Let's get signed in first, girls." Deborah laid a hand on Carole's shoulder. "Then we can check out the wagons."

They carried their bags into a large, airy lobby where stuffed buffalo and moose heads lined the wall. Whole families of other Oregon Trail trekkers bustled around the room, and Deborah and the girls had to take a place at the end of a long check-in line.

"Yes, ma'am?" the clerk said when they finally reached the front desk.

"We're the Hale party from Willow Creek, Virginia. We have reservations on Wagons West."

"Ah, yes." The clerk looked at his computer screen. "You're in the Kit Carson Suite. Fourth floor, three doors to the right of the elevator." He handed two keys to Deborah. "It's our policy to remind all our Wagons West folks that breakfast and the first orientation meeting start at five-thirty sharp, so we advise an early bedtime."

"Five-thirty in the morning?" Stevie gulped.

The clerk nodded at Stevie and smiled at Deborah. "Shall I have your luggage sent to your room? That way you and the girls can have a chance to look around the corral before dark."

"Thanks," Deborah said. "That would be great."

. They left their bags with the clerk and went back outside to get a closer look at the wagons, whose white canvas covers resembled oddly shaped ghosts in the growing darkness.

"Wow," said Stevie as she touched one of the wooden wheels. "I can't believe I'm actually touching a real covered-wagon wheel."

"I can't get over how rickety they look," said Lisa. "Can you imagine people actually packing all their possessions in one wagon and crossing rivers and prairies and mountains in it?"

Carole ran her hand along the rough canvas top of the wagon. "I wonder what they did when it got cold? This canvas doesn't look like it would be much protection from the wind and rain."

"You've got to admire the pioneers' bravery," said Deborah, staring at the wagon. "It took a lot of courage to do what they did." She smiled at the girls in the dim light. "But right now, we need to have the courage to go to bed. Five-thirty is going to come awfully early!"

They trooped back into the lodge and took the elevator up to the fourth floor. The Kit Carson Suite had two rooms, each with two double beds.

Deborah took one room for herself. "I'm going in here to call Max and let him know we arrived okay, and then I'm going to hit the sack. I'll see you three bright and early in the morning."

"Okay, Deborah," said Lisa and Carole. "Good night."

"I know you're excited, but try to get some sleep, girls. You'll need to be wide awake tomorrow."

"We will," promised Stevie.

A few minutes later, the lights were out and everyone was in bed.

"I still can't believe we're actually here," said Stevie. "Just think! Real wagons crossing the prairie to settle the West, just like they did over a hundred years ago! Cowboys, cattle rustlers, gold miners, and sodbusters!"

"Go to sleep, Stevie," said Carole.

"I can't. I'm too excited."

"You have to, Stevie. Otherwise we'll all be dead tomorrow."

"You're right." Stevie flopped back down in bed. "I promise I won't talk anymore. I just hope I can go to sleep."

"Close your eyes and count backward from a hundred," said Lisa, her voice already sounding groggy. "That always works for me."

Stevie closed her eyes. "Ninety-nine," she said to herself. "Ninety-eight . . . ninety-seven . . ."

Suddenly a loud clanging erupted in the room.

"What in the world?" Stevie sat up straight in bed, her heart pounding wildly. A funny gray light was pouring through the windows. She gasped. Was the lodge on fire?

"Lisa! Carole! Wake up!" Stevie cried, leaping out of bed and running over to the window. "I think we need to evacuate!"

She looked out the window and blinked. The funny gray light was not flames, but rather the first light of dawn coming over the mountains. And the noise she heard was not a fire alarm, but a man ringing a ranch-style triangle just below their window.

"Arggggh!" Stevie groaned. She turned back to Lisa and Carole, who were blinking at her sleepily. "Never mind. The lodge isn't on fire. This is just how they wake you up out here."

"Hi, girls!" Deborah breezed into their room, already dressed in jeans and a gingham shirt. "It's five-thirty. Time to rise and shine."

Deborah laughed as Carole and Lisa pulled the blankets back over their heads. "You guys should feel lucky. I read yesterday that the pioneer women had to get up at four o'clock to have breakfast ready by five-thirty. Think of how easy we have it! We get to sleep until almost five-thirty and breakfast is already waiting for us!"

A little while later, Stevie, Carole, and Lisa sat with all the other Oregon Trail trekkers at a long table, eating a gummy yellow corn cereal the waiters called mush.

"Is this what the pioneers ate?" Lisa whispered to Carole as she stirred the thick goop with her spoon.

"Must be," replied Carole. "I thought they ate bacon and eggs and things like that."

"It's not so bad," said Stevie, digging into her third bowl of the mush. "But of course, I'm starving."

Just then a tall, thin man with a salt-and-pepper beard came over. He wore a homespun blue shirt and a red bandanna tied around his neck. "Hi, girls," he said. "I'm Jeremy Barksdale, your wagon train leader. How do you like your breakfast?"

"It's all right," replied Stevie. "It's not Lucky Charms, but it will do."

Jeremy smiled. "Well, you know we like to make these trips authentic. Lucky Charms wasn't on the menu a hundred years ago. You're eating exactly the same thing as the pioneers."

"Yes, and Stevie's probably eating as much as the pioneers, too," said Carole, watching as Stevie polished off her third helping.

Stevie shrugged at Jeremy and her friends. "A girl's got to keep her strength up somehow."

As the trekkers continued their breakfasts, Jeremy walked over to a small platform and addressed the entire dining room.

"Hi, everybody." He held a microphone in one hand. "Welcome to Wagons West. I'm Jeremy Barksdale, and I'm your wagon train master. While you finish your breakfast, I'd like to fill you in on some historical details about the Oregon Trail and tell you some more about this trip."

He cleared his throat. "From the 1840s through the 1860s, nearly four hundred thousand pioneers crossed the western United States on what we call the Oregon Trail. It was dangerous—pioneers died from cold, hunger, cholera, and Indian attacks—and it was slow. It would take the pioneers a full week to travel the same distance we can travel by car in an hour or two today."

"Gosh," whispered Lisa. "I didn't know that."

"Despite the dangers, though, a lot of brave settlers drove these prairie schooners through knee-deep mud, raging rivers, and blinding dust storms all the way to Oregon." Jeremy smiled. "Today, I don't think we'll be in too much physical danger, but as much as possible, on Wagons West all of you will be living the authentic lives of the pioneers." He looked over his audience. "Are there any questions?"

A gray-haired man sitting in the back raised his hand. "Can you tell us about our itinerary?"

"Sure. For six days we'll travel and work just as hard as the pioneers did. At noon on the fourth day, we'll stop at Miller's Rock." He smiled knowingly at the audience. "I guarantee that by the time we stop at Miller's Rock, each of you will be a different person. You will have become the pioneers you've set out to learn about."

A murmur rippled through the crowd; then Jeremy continued. "At the end of the fifth day, we'll stop to rest at Clinchport. We'll have one day to rest up and then enjoy the rodeo going on there. Some of you may even want to participate in some of the events." He looked over the dining room. "How does that sound to everyone? Are you prepared for the challenge?"

"Sounds good to me," said Carole.

"Me too," agreed Stevie. "Although I seriously doubt we'll be turning into real pioneers."

When the dining room grew quiet again, Jeremy continued. "Now I'd like to ask each of you to introduce yourself to the group. You're going to get to know each other very well during the next six days." Jeremy looked at The Saddle Club table. "Why don't you ladies start us off?"

Deborah stood up. She had whispered to the girls before breakfast that she wasn't going to tell anybody that she was a reporter there on assignment.

"Hi, everybody." She smiled toward the other tables.

"My name is Deborah Hale and I'm from Willow Creek, Virginia. I'm taking my niece Lisa on this trip, and I'm chaperoning her and her two friends, Carole and Stevie."

Carole, Lisa, and Stevie stood and briefly introduced themselves. When they finished, Deborah stood up again. "All these girls," she added proudly, "modestly forgot to mention that they are excellent horsewomen."

"Thanks, ladies. That's great. We need all the excellent horsewomen we can get." Jeremy smiled. "Next?"

The introductions continued around the room. Sitting close to the girls were Mr. Cate, a bearded man from Alabama who played the harmonica, and Polly Shaver, a dance instructor from Ohio. There were families traveling with children younger than The Saddle Club girls and a few retired people on vacation. At one table across the room, though, a tall teenage boy arose.

"Hi, folks," he said. "My name is Gabriel. I'm also a horseback rider, and I've studied the Oregon Trail since I was in the fifth grade. I think it's terrific, the part men played in opening up the West for the future of America."

"What does he mean, *men?*" Stevie whispered to Carole and Lisa. "Women played just as important a part."

"He probably means *men* as in *people,*" Carole said.

"Yeah, Stevie," Lisa assured her. "He means *men* in the generic sense."

Stevie was about to say something else, but she looked over and saw Deborah giving them the evil eye. Reluctantly she sat back in her seat and listened to the next introduction.

A pretty little girl with long blond hair was introducing herself. "Hi. My name's Eileen. I'm eight years old. I've been looking forward to coming on this trip for months, and I'm thrilled to be going with all of you. I just know we'll all have a wonderful time!"

Everyone laughed, then applauded Eileen's enthusiasm. The last few people introduced themselves; then Jeremy spoke again.

"Thanks, everybody. Not surprisingly, this group is much like the original groups that traveled the trails— about thirty people who range in age from children to grandparents and coming from all walks of life." He glanced at a small notebook he'd been scribbling in. "While you introduced yourselves, I took some notes, and now I'd like to assign everybody a role to play."

A murmur of anticipation went through the dining room.

Jeremy looked at The Saddle Club's table. "Since Deborah's already in charge of these three young ladies, I've decided that she can be an 1840s schoolmarm who's adopted these three orphans. She's taught them their readin' and writin' and 'rithmetic, and she's taking her brood across the country to establish a school for girls in Oregon." Jeremy smiled at them. "You'll all be traveling in one wagon. Deborah, you and Stevie will drive. Carole, you'll ride a horse, and Lisa, you will be in charge of the cow."

"The cow?" Lisa's jaw dropped.

"Sure," Jeremy replied. "Our cook, Shelly Bean, has to have some way to take milk along the trail. We're not carrying any refrigerators, you know."

"Do I have to milk the cow?" asked Lisa.

Jeremy smiled. "No, Shelly will take care of the milking. You'll just have to make sure that the cow gets fed and watered and stays in good shape."

"Oh." Lisa sat back in her chair as Jeremy assigned the next people their roles. "When he said *authentic*, he wasn't kidding around."

"Shhh!" Stevie said suddenly as Jeremy pointed to Gabriel. "Let's hear what Mr. He-Man of the West gets to be!"

"Gabriel, since you're a rider and a great student of history, how about we make you assistant trail boss?"

Gabriel's face lit up with pride. "No problem," he said confidently. "I can handle that."

"I bet," scoffed Stevie. "He probably couldn't lead

this wagon train across the parking lot." She folded her arms across her chest. Then Jeremy began to speak again.

"Okay. Now that everyone's gotten a role, it's time to visit the clothes locker for your costumes and then start loading up your wagons. We're going to spend the rest of the day here at the lodge, practicing our roles and becoming accustomed to the lives we're going to be living. Then, tomorrow, it's wagons ho!" He grinned. "Good luck. And don't hesitate to holler if you need help."

Deborah and the girls rose from the table and decided to go outside and choose their wagon first. "This one looks good," said Carole, poking her head inside one that was parked under a tree. "At least I don't see any tears in the canvas where the rain could get in." She held up a horse collar. "Look, Stevie, here's the harness for the horses. Why don't you go find our team and hitch them up while Lisa and I get our costumes? We'll bring you something neat to wear."

"Okay," said Stevie. "Just don't bring me any goofy-looking old dress. I couldn't possibly drive this wagon in a skirt."

While Lisa and Carole went to get the costumes, Jeremy introduced Stevie to their team, two big bay quarter horses named Yankee and Doodle. Both walked docilely behind her as she led them back to the wagon. She had just begun to hitch them to the traces when she heard a voice behind her.

"Hey, I'll be happy to help you with that!"

Stevie turned. There, with a smug grin on his face, was Gabriel, Mr. Know-It-All since the fifth grade.

"Well, thanks, but I don't need any help with this," Stevie said as she pulled the breast collar over Doodle's head. She adjusted the collar and had to smile to herself when she saw how closely Gabriel was watching her.

"Looks like you've done that before," he said with some disappointment as Stevie slid the saddle onto Doodle's back and buckled the crupper under his tail.

"I have," replied Stevie. "Have you ever been an assistant trail boss before?"

"No." Gabriel folded his arms across his chest. "But I think I can handle it."

Stevie raised one eyebrow as she pulled the horse collar onto Yankee. "Well, if you need any help, feel free to call on me and my friends."

Gabriel gave a snide chuckle. "Thanks, but I don't think that's going to happen. Men didn't rely on the womenfolk to help them guide the wagon train."

"Yes, but the menfolk relied on women for a lot of other important jobs," said Stevie. "Like mending clothes and healing sick people and cooking meals."

She glared at Gabriel. "Maybe if you expect to eat any-thing on this trip, you ought to keep certain opinions to yourself."

Gabriel rolled his eyes. "Just my rotten luck," he muttered. "The first women's libber is going to Oregon on my wagon train."

"Maybe it's your *good* luck," Stevie whispered, hitching up Yankee and watching as Gabriel hurried over to help a family struggling with their horses' harness. "Now you can learn firsthand what womenfolk can really do!"

BY LATE AFTERNOON Stevie had shown Deborah how to steer their horses to the right by saying "gee" and to the left by calling "haw." Much to her disgust, she had also donned a long-sleeved brown dress that scratched every inch of her. Lisa was outfitted in an equally itchy blue dress with a floppy collar, while Carole, because she was a horse rider, sported a blue homespun shirt and jeans with a battered cowboy hat.

"I can't believe I have to drive this wagon across the country in a dress," Stevie complained, already scratching behind one shoulder. "Are you sure they didn't have any extra jeans?"

"I'm sure, Stevie," Carole explained for the third

time as she tried to relax on her new horse, a gray Appaloosa named Nikkia. "All the trousers were for the people who'd been assigned horses."

"I'll tell you something else you're not going to believe," called Lisa as she pulled a slow-moving white cow up to their wagon.

"What?" Stevie asked grumpily.

"This cow's name," Lisa replied.

"Let me guess," Carole said as Nikkia slapped his ears back and tossed his head. "Bossy."

"Better than that."

"Flossy," guessed Stevie, still scratching.

"Even better than that," Lisa said.

"Okay, we give up," said Carole.

"Veronica!" Lisa answered with a huge grin.

Stevie and Carole howled with laughter. Veronica di Angelo was the snobbiest, most stuck-up girl at Pine Hollow Stables. Somehow it was poetic justice that she should share her glamorous name with a stubborn cow.

"Veronica would just die if she knew someone had named a cow after her," hooted Stevie, forgetting about her scratchy dress.

"I know," Lisa laughed. "Isn't it great?"

A little while later it was time to corral the livestock for the night. Lisa took Veronica back to her pasture, while Carole gratefully pulled off Nikkia's heavy Western saddle. As Stevie began to unhitch Yankee and

Doodle, she noticed that Gabriel was leaning against a fence watching her work. For once his blue eyes sparkled in honest admiration at the smooth way she handled the horses. She was just about to say something to him when someone called him from the other end of the wagon train. She turned back to her horses, and as she returned them to the corral she realized that every time she'd seen Gabriel that day, he'd been going from wagon to wagon, pitching in wherever he was needed and generally giving people good advice.

"Well, okay, so he knows a lot," she admitted to Yankee and Doodle as they walked along beside her. "But his attitude toward 'the womenfolk' could sure be improved."

After the girls had taken care of their livestock, they decided to move from their comfortable lodge rooms out to their wagon. "If we're roughing it," said Stevie, "we ought to really rough it." Just as they were spreading their sleeping bags out on the hard wagon floor, the dinner bell rang.

"Howdy, pilgrims!" called a short, dumpy man with a grizzled beard. "My name's Shelly Bean and I'm the cook of this outfit. All who are eating out here with me need to come and get it now!"

"Let's go," said Stevie, scrambling out the back end of the wagon and nearly tripping over the hem of her long dress. "I'm starved!"

Everyone lined up. As they passed the chuck wagon, Shelly Bean grinned and ladled some odd-smelling stew onto their plates. Then they all sat in a big circle around the campfire.

"How do you like your supper?" Jeremy asked after everyone had begun to eat.

"Tastes kind of unusual," a woman said, coughing slightly.

"It's Shelly's special pemmican stew," Jeremy explained. "Dried meat and berries mixed in with cornmeal. The Cree Indians shared the recipe with the pioneers. It was a popular dish along this trail."

Everyone ate the stew. Though it was something they probably wouldn't have liked at home, here, because they were sitting around a fire in the open country and were tired from a hard day's preparation for their journey, it tasted fine.

"Are we going to be eating this every night?" someone asked Jeremy.

He shook his head. "No. We won't be lucky enough to have pemmican stew every night. Most of what we eat we'll be carrying with us, just like the pioneers. We'll be traveling the same route as them, as much as modern towns and highways permit. That means we won't have any electricity, running water, or heat. All we'll have is the outdoors and the challenge of nature."

Deborah looked guiltily over at the rucksack that

held her laptop computer. "I think I'd better leave that at the lodge," she whispered to the girls. "It won't do me any good anyway, without an outlet to recharge the batteries."

"I feel like I'm saying good-bye to the modern world forever," Lisa said, taking the last bite of her stew.

Jeremy spoke as if he'd read her mind. "Even though we're going to live the lives the pioneers lived as much as possible, I will have a cell phone, just in case of emergency. Anybody else here carrying a cell phone?"

Four people raised their hands.

"Good," said Jeremy. "We'll be well prepared. On our third night out we're scheduled to meet with some folks from a nearby dude ranch who are participating in a mock cattle drive. We'll have fresh food and a hoedown and a real celebration by the fire. It should be a lot of fun."

"It sounds terrific!" someone called from across the fire.

"I think you'll find the next six days will be an experience you won't soon forget," Jeremy said.

"I won't soon forget spending six days in this dumb dress," grumbled Stevie, trying to scratch between her shoulder blades.

After everyone had finished supper, Stevie, Carole, and Lisa helped wash the dishes. Then they sponged themselves off in the cold, rushing creek and walked slowly toward their wagon.

"I can't believe how tired I am, and it's not even sundown!" Carole said.

"I know." Lisa yawned. "That sleeping bag is going to feel great."

"I've got to write in my journal some before I go to sleep," Stevie said as the girls climbed into the back of the wagon.

"Are you sure you've got the energy for that?" Carole asked.

"Well, I am tired, but I made Phil a promise and I'm going to keep it."

The girls settled in next to Deborah, who was already in her sleeping bag. Stevie lit a small oil lamp and dug her pen and journal out of her backpack.

"Don't write too late, Stevie," said Deborah from under her covers. "Remember, the real journey starts tomorrow at sunup."

"I won't," Stevie whispered. She sat up and balanced the journal on her legs. *Day One*, she wrote at the top of the first page.

Today we had a breakfast of mush and met our wagon master, Jeremy Barksdale. We've also met our horses and our cow and one very stuck-up boy named

Gabriel, who thinks men conquered the West all by themselves.

Stevie started to write that Gabriel did know all about wagons and harnesses and packing supplies, but she decided Phil probably wouldn't be interested in that. Instead, she wrote:

Gabriel is tall and lean, with dark brown hair and deep blue eyes. Occasionally he will smile, and then he has a dimple in his right cheek.

"Oh no," Stevie whispered, feeling a hot blush of embarrassment as she read over her words. "I can't say that!" Quickly she tore the page out of her journal and started again.

Today we had a breakfast of mush and met our wagon master, Jeremy Barksdale. We've met our horses and our cow and one very stuck-up boy named Gabriel, who thinks men conquered the West all by themselves. He considers himself an expert on everything from wagon driving to sheepherding, but I wonder how much he really knows. It should be fun to see how well he does with his job of assistant trail boss.

Stevie reread her words and smiled. This was better. This was more like the real Gabriel. She added a few paragraphs about their wagon and the campfire; then she was done for the evening. She stuffed her journal back into her bag, blew out the lamp, and curled into her sleeping bag. In an instant she was asleep.

IT WAS A little past midnight when Deborah shook Carole and Lisa awake. "Girls, there's an emergency phone call for me at the lodge. You sit tight and I'll be back as soon as I can."

"Okay," Lisa mumbled, rubbing her eyes.

By the time Deborah had climbed over the sleeping bags and out of the wagon, all three girls were wide awake.

"What do you think it could be?" Carole asked as she watched Deborah and Jeremy hurry toward the lodge.

"I hope nothing's wrong with Maxi," said Stevie.

"Or Max," added Lisa.

For what seemed like forever, they huddled in the dark wagon, wondering what could have gone wrong. Finally Deborah reappeared.

"Okay, girls, here's the deal. My father was in a car accident this evening. He's in a hospital right now, and though it looks like he's going to be okay, my mom's really upset. Since I'm an only child, I have to be there for both of them. I hope you won't be too disappointed, but I'm afraid we'll have to leave right away."

"Sure, Deborah. We understand. We would want to be there if any of our parents were hurt," said Carole, trying to hide her disappointment.

"Jeremy's making our flight arrangements, so I guess the best thing for us to do is to pack our stuff up and go back to the lodge. I'm really sorry this had to happen."

"Don't worry about it, Deborah," said Lisa. "This would have been a great trip, but we can do it some other time."

"Thanks. I appreciate your understanding." Deborah gave a tired sigh.

They had just begun to roll up their sleeping bags when Jeremy appeared at the back of the wagon.

"Hey, Deborah, I was thinking. I watched these girls all day today and I think they're all extremely capable, mature young ladies. It would be a shame to have them come this far and then have to leave. Why don't you let me take them under my personal wing for the rest of the trip? That is, if it's okay with you."

Deborah blinked. "Well, it's okay with me if it's okay with them. And, of course, with their parents."

"It's okay with us," Stevie assured her.

"Well, let's go call everybody in Virginia and explain the situation."

An hour later, the girls stood with Deborah in the lobby of the lodge. They had all gotten permission from their parents to remain on the trip, and they were waiting with Deborah for the cab that was to take her back to the airport.

"It's too bad I'm not going to be able to write that article," Deborah said as she leaned against a long leather sofa. "That was the whole reason we came out here in the first place."

"Oh, don't worry about that, Deborah," Carole said. "Lisa and Stevie and I can do all the research you could possibly want. Stevie's even keeping a journal."

"That's right," said Stevie. "We can help you write the article when we get back."

Lisa gave Deborah a hug. "It's the least we can do."

"Well, thanks, girls," Deborah said, hugging each of them. "I appreciate your good intentions."

"No, really," insisted Stevie. "We can be a big help. I know we can."

Just then the cab pulled up.

"I've got to go," said Deborah, grabbing her backpack. "You girls be careful and do what Jeremy tells you. I'll see you in about a week!"

The Saddle Club waved as the cab pulled away from the lodge, leaving them standing alone with ten covered wagons under a dark sky spangled with stars.

6

"STEVIE! WAKE UP!" Carole reined in Nikkia and peered at Stevie, who was nodding in the driver's seat of the wagon. Breakfast was over, and everyone was waiting to pull out.

"I'm not asleep," Stevie said, yawning. "I'm just resting my eyes. I never could get back to sleep after Deborah left."

"Me neither," said Lisa, who stood on the other side of the wagon holding Veronica by a frazzled rope. Lisa rubbed her eyes. "I think I got about fifteen minutes of sleep the entire night. I couldn't believe it when the triangle rang at five-thirty. This is going to be one long day!"

Stevie blinked at Jeremy, who had ridden to the front of the column. Suddenly she sat up straight and tightened the reins. "I'm not sure, but I think our long day might be starting right now."

The girls looked toward the lead wagon. Jeremy, on a big brown-and-white paint horse, stood to one side of it. He waited for everyone's attention, then rose in his stirrups.

"Everyone ready?" he called, lifting his hat high above his head and grinning broadly.

Everyone in the wagon train cheered.

"Then wagons ho!" he called. His horse rose up once on its hind legs, then turned quickly around. With a swish of its tail, it carried Jeremy westward at a brisk trot. One by one, the wagons began to lumber after him.

"Here we go!" Stevie cried when their turn to move came. She popped Yankee and Doodle's reins. The horses strained hard against their collars. Then all at once The Saddle Club began to roll west.

The morning was a busy one. Stevie itched constantly from the rough material of her dress, and the wagon bumped her rear end with every turn of the wheels. The sun beamed down on the back of her neck, and though Yankee and Doodle pulled the wagon easily, they paid far more attention to the team in front of them than they did to Stevie.

Lisa spent the morning trying to control Veronica, who tended to stop every ten feet to graze leisurely by the side of the road.

"Come on, Veronica," Lisa would coo sweetly, giving a gentle tug on the rope. "We need to walk this way, over by the wagons." Veronica would look dully at Lisa, take one step, then pull up a mouthful of grass as the wagon train rolled past them. "Come on, sweet Veronica," Lisa would call again, tugging harder. Veronica would chew her grass and budge only an inch. Finally, as the dust from the passing wagons began to sting Lisa's eyes and clog her nose, she took a deep breath and gave a mighty heave on Veronica's rope. "Come on, you nitwit cow!" she commanded. At that, Veronica bawled a low *moo* and began to trudge forward.

Though she was sleepy, Carole was able to endure Nikkia's rough trot all morning. She could tell by the way the stocky Appaloosa slapped his ears back when she asked for a canter that he had been the victim of a lot of what she called kick-and-yank riders. As she looked around, she saw that many of the people riding with the wagon train were that kind of rider.

"If you pull the right rein gently, then release it, he'll go more willingly," she finally told Karen Nicely, a woman whose horse was so confused by her aids that he had just stopped, unable to figure out which way she wanted him to go.

"Thanks," Karen Nicely said, trying what Carole had suggested.

"Hey, how do you make them stop?" asked a breathless man whose horse was jigging sideways.

"And how do you make them back up?" called someone else.

Suddenly Carole found herself giving mini–riding lessons, right there in the middle of the trail. She didn't mind, because she didn't want any novice riders abusing their horses from lack of knowledge. Still, showing everybody what to do as the wagons rolled around them was exhausting. *I never realized before what a good job Max does of teaching,* she thought as she and Nikkia were finally able to canter back up to Stevie and the wagon.

They stopped for lunch at midday. Stevie pulled the team to a halt while Carole fetched water for Veronica and their three horses. Lisa tugged Veronica up to the wagon and tied her to the rear wheel. After they had taken care of their animals, they trudged over to the chow line.

"How's it going for you girls?" Jeremy asked as he strode past.

Stevie yawned. "Fine, except I've got blisters on my rear from the wagon, and blisters on my fingers from the reins, plus neither Yankee nor Doodle is paying me a whole lot of attention."

"And Veronica pays me no attention at all," added Lisa.

Jeremy grinned. "Great. This is exactly what the pioneers had to deal with—cranky cows and hardmouthed horses. You're getting a real taste of history!"

"Right now, I'd rather get a real taste of lunch!" said Carole as Jeremy ran over to assist a family whose wagon wheel needed to be greased.

Shelly Bean worked hard ladling out the fried cornmeal mush and fresh apples he'd fixed for lunch. "Eat hearty!" he called as the girls took their plates and sat down beside a small pond. The mush and apples seemed like a peculiar lunch, but they tasted wonderful, and soon they felt their usual energy levels returning.

"I'm beginning to understand why they assigned four people to a wagon," Stevie said, rubbing the blisters on her hand. "Taking care of a wagon plus three horses and a cow is a tough job for four people, let alone three."

"Don't forget that Jeremy is always here to help us," Carole said.

"Oh, I think we'll be fine, but it's exhausting doing all these jobs by ourselves." Lisa wiped the dust from her forehead. "Why don't we change places every few hours? The jobs won't get any easier, but at least we'll exercise different parts of our anatomies. Stevie, you won't get bounced so badly; Carole, your legs won't be so sore; and maybe one of you will have better luck with the cow."

"That's a good idea," agreed Stevie. "Although I don't think any of us would have much luck with anything named Veronica."

After lunch they resumed their jobs, agreeing to switch off in an hour. Stevie pulled on a pair of leather gloves she'd thrown into her backpack, so the blisters on her fingers bothered her less. Once again Jeremy rode to the head of the column, waved his hat, and shouted, "Wagons ho!" And once again they were off.

The wagons rolled westward onto the vast plains. Miles of flat, nearly treeless land stretched to the horizon. As far as the girls could see, the long green grass was dotted with small purple wildflowers. Little yellow birds Polly Shaver called western meadowlarks chat-. tered to each other, and the delicious smell of earth and new grass drifted on the warm breeze.

"This doesn't look much like Virginia, does it?" Stevie commented as Lisa tugged Veronica along.

"No, but it's just as pretty." Lisa looked out over the prairie. "It's pretty in a flatter, more open way."

"I wonder how far away we can see." Carole squinted at the distant horizon from atop Nikkia's back.

"Maybe fifty miles," guessed Stevie. "After all, these are the wide-open spaces."

Suddenly Veronica stopped dead in her tracks. She twisted her head around and pulled up a mouthful of grass. "Looks like it's Veronica's snack time." Lisa shrugged at Stevie as the wagon rumbled past her. "We'll catch up to you later."

"Okay." Stevie scratched under the collar of her dress. "See you soon."

She and Carole rolled on until a voice came from the rear of the train. "Hey, Carole! Can you help me with this horse?"

Carole looked over her shoulder to see a desperate-looking man on an equally desperate-looking pinto waving at her. "I think someone needs a riding lesson," she said to Stevie as she turned Nikkia and began to trot toward the man. "I'll be back in a few minutes!"

"Don't teach him anything I wouldn't teach him!" warned Stevie with a laugh.

Stevie drove on, content to let the sun warm her face as Yankee and Doodle followed the wagon ahead of them.

"Hi!" she heard a small voice call.

She looked down. Beside her wagon skipped the pretty little blond girl who'd charmed everyone at their get-acquainted breakfast.

"Hi," said Stevie. "You're Eileen, aren't you?"

"Yes." Eileen smiled. She held up a straw basket filled

with angel-shaped cookies. "My mother baked these cookies and we were wondering if you'd like one."

"Sure," said Stevie. She reached down and grabbed a cookie from the basket. "Thanks."

"It's neat that you can drive a wagon and eat at the same time," Eileen said admiringly.

"Oh, it's not too hard," Stevie replied, her mouth full. "Would you like to learn how to drive?"

"Sure." Eileen's eyes were bright.

"Then climb up here and I'll show you." Stevie reached down to help her onto the wagon. In a moment Eileen was sitting beside her.

"Okay, Eileen. Here's what you do. Put the left rein over the index finger of your left hand, then put the right rein under your middle finger." Stevie helped Eileen arrange the reins in her hand. "Then hold your hand right at your belly button with your knuckles facing the horses."

Eileen positioned her hand as Stevie had showed her. "Is that all?" She looked up at Stevie with pale green eyes.

"Just about," said Stevie.

Eileen frowned as Yankee and Doodle trudged along. "How could you make them go faster?"

"Oh, you just pop a whip over their heads, or you pop the reins, if you haven't got a whip."

"Like this?" Eileen took the long ends of the reins

and gave both horses a sudden, vicious swat on their rumps.

"No!" Stevie cried, but it was too late. Yankee whinnied and reared in the traces, and then both horses surged forward at a gallop.

The jolt somersaulted Eileen backward into the wagon and loosened the reins in her hand. Stevie had just enough time to grab them before they fell between the horses' thundering feet. Quickly she grasped them in her left hand and braced herself against the footboard of the wagon. "Whoa!" she called, pulling hard on the reins. "Whoa!"

The horses did not stop. They galloped straight for the wagon in front of them, where a little boy sat in the back, a look of terror on his face. Stevie realized she would have to turn the team quickly if she was to avoid a real disaster.

"Haw!" she cried as loudly as she could, using both hands to turn the horses to the left. "Haw, Yankee! Haw, Doodle!"

The horses drew closer. Just as they were about to lunge into the wagon, Doodle pulled to the left. Yankee followed. Stevie's wagon flew past the other wagon in a blur, stirring up a huge cloud of yellow dust.

"Hey!" Stevie heard an angry voice shout over the sound of other horses whinnying. "No racing! You're messing up the order of the train!"

"I'm not racing!" Stevie said through gritted teeth as she pulled back on the reins with all her strength. "I'm trying to stop!"

Finally Yankee and Doodle slowed to a trot, and Stevie managed to pull them to a stop just as they drew up even with the lead wagon. For a moment it was all she could do just to breathe through the thick dust.

"Everything okay here?" Jeremy galloped up on his paint, frowning.

"Fine, now," gasped Stevie, red-faced and still out of breath.

"Well, take your place back in line when you can," he said firmly as he turned back to the head of the column.

"Just a minute." Stevie heard a small voice behind her. Eileen scrambled out from inside the wagon and climbed to the ground. "Some driving teacher you are," she said, glaring up at Stevie. "Look what you did to my angel cookies!" She held up the basket of broken cookies for Stevie to see.

"Well, gosh, so sorry," Stevie muttered. She started to add that she and Eileen could have wound up as crumbled as the cookies, but Eileen was already running back to the other wagons. Stevie shook her head and pulled Yankee and Doodle around, waiting to take her place in the line. As she waited, she watched Eileen run up and down the wagon train, showing everybody her broken cookies and pointing at Stevie.

"Some little angel you turned out to be," Stevie whispered. "From now on it'll just be heavenly if you stay away from me."

7

WHEN THE THICK yellow dust finally settled, Stevie saw her old place in the line and maneuvered the horses back into it. The little boy still looked out the back of the wagon she followed, only now he shook his finger at Stevie, as if she'd done something very bad.

Stevie wanted to make a face at the kid, but instead she gave him a sweet smile and kept Yankee and Doodle at a safe distance. There was no point in acting like a jerk to a little kid who didn't realize what had really happened. She took a deep breath and was trying to relax back into the bumpy rhythm of the wagon when she saw Gabriel riding toward her. He sat easily in the saddle as his bay horse loped along, and he wore his cowboy hat tilted forward on his head.

"You need to keep these horses in line," he said, reining up beside her. "We ride this way for a reason. And green drivers like you shouldn't be trying to race. It makes the other horses nervous and scares everybody on the wagons."

"Green drivers?" Stevie squawked, barely believing her ears. This arrogant tinhorn thought she was green!

"Yeah. Green drivers. No experienced driver would have done what you did. You can harness horses up okay, but I don't think you know a thing about driving them." He gave her a tight smile. "Just keep in line and follow the wagon in front of you. Do that and you'll be fine."

Stevie glared at him. She wanted to explain what had really happened, but she was so angry she could barely speak. "Well, thanks for your advice, Mr. Assistant Trail Boss," she finally managed to say. "I never would have figured it out all by myself."

"Just trying to help a lady." Smugly Gabriel tipped his hat and turned his horse back to the front of the line.

Stevie was so furious she thought she might explode. *What an idiot!* she fumed silently as she watched him ride away. *He's as bad as the kid in the next wagon. They both think they know exactly what happened when they know nothing at all!*

After Stevie had counted to ten several times, she calmed down enough to enjoy the rest of the afternoon. Yankee and Doodle pulled the wagon steadily, and as the sun began to set behind the far hills, Jeremy waved his hat around his head, the signal for everyone to circle up for the night. Stevie pulled into place and the girls began to work at making their camp. Stevie unhitched the team, fed them, and turned them out in the makeshift corral. Lisa watered Veronica and hitched her to the wagon wheel while Carole unsaddled Nikkia and gave him a good brushing. When they had finished taking care of their livestock, they wearily washed the gritty dust from their faces in a small creek and decided it might be a good night to sleep under the stars.

"I understand now why the pioneers turned in early," said Carole as she pulled her sleeping bag out of the wagon.

"Why?" asked Lisa.

"Because look at all this work we've done just to get ready to go to bed, and we still have to help with supper."

"I know," said Stevie, grabbing her own sleeping bag

and wincing from the blisters on her fingers. "I sure do miss Deborah. She would have been an extra pair of hands."

After the girls had joined some other campers in helping Shelly Bean with dinner, they took their seats around the campfire. Mr. Cate played his harmonica while Jeremy sat on a log, telling more history of the Oregon Trail.

"In the early 1800s, Lewis and Clark, helped by the Shoshone woman Sacagawea, charted the trail to the Northwest. After that, there was a big dispute over whether the land there really belonged to England or the United States. In 1841 the first group of settlers left the banks of the Missouri River and headed west toward the promised land of Oregon." Jeremy gazed into the crackling fire. "Those pioneers pushed the western boundary of America to the Pacific Ocean, and Oregon joined the union in 1859."

The girls' eyes glowed with admiration at what these brave pioneers had accomplished so many years before, and they listened carefully as Jeremy spoke of some of the more famous settlers who might have camped in that very spot. Finally, as the embers of the fire began to die, Lisa yawned and stood up.

"I don't know about you guys, but I'm beat," she said. "My shoulders hurt from tugging Veronica, my feet hurt from walking, and my legs hurt from doing everything else. I'm going to bed."

"Me too," said Carole, joining her in a yawn. "All the same parts of me ache as well. How about you, Stevie?"

"Count me in." Stevie got up slowly. "And ditto on the body parts. I sure wish we had a big feather bed to sleep in."

The girls walked over to their wagon. They had just arranged their sleeping bags on a soft bit of ground when Jeremy walked up.

"Hi, girls." He took off his cowboy hat. "I wanted to let you know that I just got a call from Deborah on my cell phone. She got back to Virginia safely and she's with her parents. Her dad's got a few broken bones and he's real sore, but he's going to be fine. And her mother's much calmer now that Deborah's there."

"That's wonderful news," said Carole.

Jeremy nodded. "She said to tell you three to be brave pioneers."

"Hey, speaking of being brave pioneers," Stevie said suddenly, "I'd like to explain what happened today, Jeremy. I wasn't trying to race with the other wagons. I was just showing that little girl Eileen how to hold the reins when she slapped both horses on their rumps. Yankee reared and bolted, and Doodle took off right along with him. I'm sorry if I scared the other people on the wagon train."

Jeremy's eyes grew serious. "Stevie, you don't need to apologize. I saw the whole thing. You were trying to be nice to Eileen, and you simply misjudged her capacity for misbehavior. I thought you did a fine job of getting your team back under control. You're probably one of the few people on this trip who could have done that."

Stevie began to blush. "Thanks."

Jeremy smiled and put his hat back on. "Well, you girls get a good night's sleep. You know how early five-thirty comes."

"Good night, Jeremy," they called as he walked over to his own camp.

The girls climbed into their sleeping bags. Above them, filmy clouds floated across the moon, and the sounds of Mr. Cate's harmonica floated over the campsite. Stevie lit her tiny oil lamp and pulled her journal from beneath her pillow.

"Stevie, are you writing again tonight?" Carole yawned.

"Just for a few minutes," replied Stevie. She read over what she'd written the night before, then turned to a fresh page. *Day Two*, she wrote at the top.

Today was very exciting. Yankee and Doodle ran away with the wagon. Though it was really scary, I got them back under control. Then Mr. Know-It-All Gabriel rode up and told me that I was a green driver who didn't know anything. I was furious! He is the most arrogant, obnoxious person I've ever met. But when he told me how I really didn't know what I was doing, his eyes turned this deep shade of blue, and when he rode away, he sat on the horse like his legs had been made for the saddle. And he wears his cowboy hat this really neat way that makes him look so cool.

"Wait a minute." Stevie blinked, rereading the words she'd just written. "This isn't what I wanted to say at all." She stared at the writing and wondered if she should cross it out or just start all over on a fresh page. Finally she tore the page out of the book and wadded it into a ball. *I'll toss that one into the campfire tomorrow morning,* she thought as she rolled over to sleep. *And maybe overnight I'll think of what I really want to say.*

From her own sleeping bag, Lisa heard Stevie rip the page from her book and then turn over to go to sleep. She smiled. *Stevie must be having a hard time driving a wagon all day and writing about it at night.* Lisa didn't blame her. She felt as if she was having a hard time doing everything from keeping up with Veronica to washing her face in the cold, muddy creeks. She sighed. How wonderful it would be to jump into a steaming hot shower and then into a soft, cozy bed. *You must be more*

73

like your mother than you thought, a little voice whispered to her just as she was falling asleep. *All these modern comforts are as important to you as they are to her.*

No, they're not, Lisa protested sleepily. *Showers and beds and indoor toilets aren't important at all when you can look at the stars at night and smell the breeze that blows over the plains and listen to meadowlarks singing in the trees.* The little voice kept whispering, though, until Lisa finally rolled over in her sleeping bag and pulled the blankets to her chin. Just as she felt herself falling into a deep and restful sleep, something cold and wet splashed on her cheek. She opened her eyes. Another wet something hit her, then another after that. She sat up. A gentle but insistent rain had begun to fall.

"Stevie! Carole! Wake up!" Lisa shook her friends. "It's raining. We need to get under some shelter."

Fumbling in the dark, the girls got up, pulled their sleeping bags beneath the wagon, and settled down again to sleep. The ground was a lot harder under the wagon, and what felt like a dozen small rocks dug into Lisa's back. *Be brave*, she told herself, twisting and turning as she tried to get comfortable. *The pioneers had to cope with rain and pain and tiredness, and you can, too.*

"IS ANYBODY AWAKE but me?" Lisa rose up on one elbow and peered through the dim light.

"I am," muttered Carole. "I woke up when that darn prairie chicken started chirping."

"I'm not." Stevie's voice was muffled by her sleeping bag. "I'm having a nightmare that I'm awake. I'm actually still sound asleep."

Lisa ran one hand through her short, sun-streaked hair. "I don't know about you guys, but I don't think I slept a wink all night. It felt like a small river was flowing underneath me."

Stevie sat up and felt the underside of her sleeping

bag. "I think we must have slept downhill from some runoff," she said. "My sleeping bag is soggy."

"Let's get dressed," said Carole. "That way at least our outside clothes will help get us warm and dry."

Lisa watched as Stevie and Carole scrambled out from under the wagon; then she followed them. The night before, her arms had ached from tugging Veronica along. Now her back was sore from having slept on the rocky ground. As she slowly pulled her sleeping bag from beneath the wagon, she wished, for an instant, that this wagon train reenactment was over and that she was back in civilization, sleeping in a soft bed in warm, dry pajamas.

You really are like your mother, the little voice chirped inside her head.

No, I'm not, she argued silently. *I left all those spoiled ideas back in Virginia, just like I left my suitcases stashed in Stevie's closet.*

I don't think so, said the singsong voice. *Yes, I did,* Lisa insisted, refusing to listen anymore. She threw her sleeping bag into the wagon and climbed up after it. She was determined not to complain about anything that day, especially things as silly as wet clothes and a sore back.

"Yuck," Stevie said as she pulled her dress on over her head. "This scratchy old dress feels awful against my skin."

"I know." Carole buttoned her blue shirt. "And this wagon is so dark you can barely see what you're putting on." She zipped her jeans. "I don't guess that matters, though, since we only have one outfit to wear."

"Oh, it's not so bad." Lisa tried her best to sound cheerful. "I mean, the pioneers had to dress in here, and their wagons were a lot more crowded with stuff than ours is." She held up her blue dress and noticed that the hem was covered with mud and that dust had settled in the fringes around the collar. "After all, we're here to get a taste of what pioneer life was like. They didn't have umbrellas and hair dryers and microwaves. All they had was what they could carry, and they couldn't carry much in these little wagons."

"Right now I wish this one was carrying a nice hot shower," said Stevie.

"Maybe if we don't complain it won't seem so bad." Lisa pulled her dress on. "You know, keep a stiff upper lip and everything. After all, we've got a job to do." She sat down and began to put on her shoes. "In fact, we've got several jobs to do. We've got to learn all about the trip and the land, and do our research for Deborah's article, and take care of our animals, plus all the other basic stuff, like surviving."

"And like not letting Gabriel get under our skin." Stevie pushed up the sleeves of her dress and frowned. "He is such a creep."

"He is pretty arrogant," Carole agreed, tying her long hair in a ponytail.

"Watch out, then." Lisa looked out the back of the wagon. "Here comes Mr. Arrogant Creep now."

Gabriel sauntered up to the back of their wagon. "Hi," he said, smiling his funny, lopsided smile. "How are you ladies doing this morning?"

"Fine," snapped Stevie, her hazel eyes flashing.

"Well," he said, laughing, "you're the only girls on this trip who are. Every other female I've talked to this morning has only complained about the weather. 'It was soooo nasty last night,'" he mimicked in a high voice. "'All my clothes got wet and my hair's a mess! I miss my hair dryer!'" Gabriel gave a snort. "I think this trip might be too tough for girls, if all they can do is whine about one night of light rain!"

Carole and Lisa felt Stevie twitch between them. They knew how infuriating Gabriel's words were to her. Lisa quickly shifted in front of her while Carole grabbed the back of her dress. It would do no good for Stevie to pounce on Gabriel like a mountain lion in front of the whole camp!

Gabriel continued, obviously unaware that he had insulted The Saddle Club and every other female on the trip. "Anyway, I won't have to put up with any slackers today. As assistant trail boss, I get to ride with

one of the scouts to make sure the trail ahead is clear."
He smiled at the girls and tipped his hat. "So I hope
you ladies have a nice, dry, comfy day!"

"It's looking sunnier already," Stevie called as Gabriel strolled over toward Jeremy's camp.

When he was out of sight, the girls turned back inside their wagon.

"Can you believe him?" Stevie clenched her fists in
frustration.

"No." Carole shook her head. "Actually, I can't."

"Boy, I can think of about a hundred jokes I'd like to
play on him. Starting with greasing his saddle so that he
can't stay on his horse and then gluing the inside of his
stupid old hat so that he can't tip it to the 'ladies'
anymore!"

"Stevie!" Lisa warned. "You could get into some serious trouble if you started playing your practical jokes
here."

"I know," Stevie replied, realizing that she had to
behave. "Getting into trouble would be bad; Deborah is
counting on us." She sighed; then she looked at Carole
and Lisa and smiled. "Anyway, there are so many wonderful things going on here, how could I possibly be
thinking about getting into trouble?"

"Wonderful things?" Lisa raised one eyebrow. "Like
what?"

Stevie grinned. "Like we're here in the middle of this beautiful country reenacting this wonderful piece of history!"

"Well, yes," Lisa agreed. "And apparently we're the only females on this wagon train who aren't complaining about it."

"Right!" said Stevie. "See how much better things are already? And we won't have to deal with that jerk Gabriel for the rest of the day! He'll be out of our hair until the campfire tonight, and that's the most wonderful thing imaginable!"

The girls hopped out of the wagon to find that the day was sunny and bright. The night's rain had washed the mugginess out of the air, and everything sparkled as if it were brand new. They ate their mush for breakfast, then broke camp with everyone else. Stevie hitched up Yankee and Doodle more smoothly than she ever had before, and Carole found Nikkia's trot a lot easier to sit. And though Lisa was sore from her night underneath the wagon, Veronica seemed well rested and had caught on to the fact that she was supposed to walk with them instead of wandering around the plains munching grass.

The Saddle Club moved up one place in line and headed west. With Gabriel scouting ahead of them and bratty Eileen remaining with her own family, they had a good morning. Stevie and Lisa switched jobs once, and Lisa was about to trade off driving with Carole when Jeremy halted the train for lunch.

"Thank goodness!" said Lisa as she pulled Yankee and Doodle to a stop. "I was just hoping we would break for lunch."

Carole glanced over at her friend and noticed dark circles underneath her eyes. "Lisa, you're looking a little tired," she said. "Why don't you take a nap after lunch? Stevie and I can handle your share of the chores, and I'll volunteer to milk Veronica for anybody who would like some fresh milk."

Lisa's mouth fell open. "Where did you learn to milk a cow?"

"Oh, it's part of Marine Corps basic training," Carole replied, then burst out laughing at Lisa's astonished expression. "Actually, I learned on my aunt's farm in Minnesota. They have a holstein named Cora Mae."

Lisa smiled in gratitude. "Carole, that would be wonderful. I could use a little extra sleep."

"And I bet some of these pioneers could use a glass of milk!"

After lunch Stevie helped clean up while Lisa retreated to the wagon for a nap. Though Carole's own arms and legs ached from riding and driving, she tied Veronica to one of the few trees growing nearby and sat down on a milking stool beside her. A small crowd of pioneers gathered around to watch.

"Okay, Veronica," Carole said to the cow, which turned and gave her a dubious look. "Let's show these people what you can do."

Hoping that she hadn't forgotten all the milking skills she'd learned in Minnesota, Carole placed a bucket beneath the cow and gave one of her udders a pull and a squeeze. Veronica shifted once on her feet; then suddenly a stream of white milk began to clatter into the bucket. A cheer went up from the crowd.

"Wow, Carole," said Polly Shaver. "That's neat."

"Yeah," a man agreed. "We didn't think you could really do it."

Carole smiled. "Actually, Veronica's the one doing most of it. I'm just sort of at the right place at the right time."

"Can I have a taste?" a little boy asked.

"Sure," said Carole. "Let me get this bucket a little fuller."

Veronica gave a half bucket of milk. Everybody who wanted some got some.

Awhile later Lisa climbed out of the wagon, looking rested and refreshed. "Did Veronica do okay?" she asked, looking at the cow, which had again wandered off to browse in the grass.

"She was the hit of the day." Carole grinned.

"Thanks for helping me out like that, Carole," said Lisa. "I feel so much better."

"Well, that's what The Saddle Club is all about," said Carole.

"Maybe that's what the pioneer spirit is all about, too," said Stevie, who had just finished the milk she'd scooped from Carole's bucket. "Anyway, now we need to get going. The train's rolling west."

They resumed their old jobs, but this time with lighter hearts. Though they still had their various aches and pains, they rode along thinking that problems didn't seem nearly as bad when you were with people who shared them right along with you, and who were happy to help you whenever they could.

9

THAT EVENING A crimson sunset blazed in the western sky. Stevie and Carole and Lisa sat enjoying it beside the campfire as they finished the last of their supper. Just as the sun finally slipped behind the distant mountains, Mr. Cate began to play a soft tune on his harmonica and Jeremy stood up to start their nightly campfire session.

"Tonight, instead of talking about the history of the Oregon Trail, we're going to do something a little different," he announced with a devilish gleam in his eye. "We're going to do what the pioneers often did after a long, hard day on the trail."

"What's that?" someone asked from across the fire.

Jeremy grinned. "We're going to entertain each other with stories. Tall tales, jokes, riddles, anything you want. It's all up to you."

Stevie winked at Lisa and Carole as she raised her hand. "Hey, Jeremy, can we tell ghost stories?"

"We sure can," he replied. "Are you volunteering to tell the first one?"

"Why, yes," Stevie said. "As a matter of fact, I am."

"Then stand up here by the fire so that everyone can hear you, and scare us to death." Jeremy led the campers in a round of applause as Stevie approached the fire. "Ladies and gentlemen, the best ghost-story teller in Virginia, Ms. Stevie Lake."

Stevie bowed deeply and began her story. Though Lisa and Carole had heard it many times before—the legend of a ghost stallion that seeks revenge on the drovers who rounded up his herd—that night Stevie changed the setting from Virginia to the Western plains and transformed the Chincoteague Island ponies to wild mustangs. Everyone's eyes grew wide as Stevie described the terror of the drovers who kept hearing ghostly hoofbeats bearing down upon them when there was nothing there. Finally, just as Stevie reached the climax of her story, one of the real wagon train horses let out a single shrill scream. Everybody nearly jumped out of their skin.

"And the stallion lives on to this day," Stevie finished with a flourish, "still searching for anyone who has ever hurt a horse. That might even be him right now, looking for you!"

Except for two people, everyone burst into applause. To Stevie's delight, little Eileen sat trembling in her mother's lap, her arms clutching her mother's neck in terror. Gabriel, on the other hand, had pushed his cowboy hat back on his head and was giving Stevie a curious, unreadable look.

"Thank you, Stevie," said Jeremy. "That was great. Anybody else have an entertainment for the evening?"

"I do," Gabriel announced.

"Let's have it, then," said Jeremy.

Stevie sat down, shrugging at Carole and Lisa as Gabriel sauntered to the middle of the circle.

"Does everyone realize this is Crow country?" Gabriel began. He stood in the circle and began talking about an Indian brave who'd killed his blood brother. He hadn't spoken a minute before Stevie realized that this was a ghost story, too. Gabriel was trying to one-up her! Not only did he think he knew everything about horses and wagons and the Oregon Trail, he thought he was the best ghost-story teller on the planet as well. *No way,* Stevie silently vowed as Gabriel spoke in eerie tones over the fire. *I'm a hundred times better than he is, and I'll prove it if I have to tell ghost stories all night.*

Gabriel ended his tale with a war whoop, which again made everyone jump and made little Eileen cover her ears.

"Anybody else?" Jeremy asked after Gabriel sat down.

"I've got another," Stevie called out, giving Gabriel a steely glare. "And it's the scariest story in the world!"

"Go, Stevie!" another camper called. "We want some more of yours!"

"Okay, Stevie, you're on again." Jeremy laughed and sat down. Everyone's eyes turned to Stevie.

"Once upon a time," she began, standing close to the fire so that the flames would make her cheeks and chin look scary, "there was a young man who feared rats more than anything in the world. . . ."

A hush fell on the campers as Stevie wove her tale of murder and revenge. Little Eileen began to cry, and as Stevie's voice rose in conclusion, all the campers gazed at her in rapt attention.

"And every time you hear scratching that you can't explain, just remember that man and what the rats did to him!"

Everybody murmured approval when the story was over, and Stevie sat down to great applause.

"Wow, Stevie, I've heard you tell that one before, but never that well." Carole rubbed her arms and shivered. "You really gave me the chills."

"Yeah, Stevie, that was great!" Lisa said with a smile.

Gabriel was halfway back to the campfire when Jeremy stopped him. "I'm afraid that's all we have time for tonight. We've got a big day tomorrow. We're going to be crossing the river, plus tomorrow night the dude ranchers are going to be joining us. I think right now all of us had better call it a day and get a good night's sleep."

The campers stretched their legs and got up slowly, yawning as they made their way to their sleeping bags. Several people congratulated Stevie on her storytelling as they went to their own campsites.

"Where shall we sleep tonight?" asked Carole when the girls reached their wagon. "Inside, outside, or underneath the wagon?"

Lisa looked up at the twinkling stars. "Oh, let's sleep outside. The ground is softer than the wagon floor, and there's not a cloud in the sky. It couldn't possibly rain again."

They pulled their sleeping bags to a grassy little dip in the ground and settled in. After Lisa and Carole had said good night, Stevie lit the oil lamp and reached for her journal. Her body was tired, but her mind was still wide awake from all the fun she'd had.

Day Three

Today was the best day yet. After a rainy, sleepless night, we woke up to beautiful weather. All our work went a lot easier, and we traded off jobs several times during the afternoon. After lunch Carole milked the cow and gave everyone fresh milk. At the campfire tonight I told two of my favorite ghost stories. The last one scared that little creep Eileen so much she began to cry, but I don't care. After her stunt with the horses, it's exactly what she deserves. Most of the people on this trip are really nice, and the campfire tonight was the most fun yet.

She read over her words and smiled. This journal had been a great idea. She could read these pages when she was eighty and remember what a wonderful time she'd had. She stuffed the little book under her pillow and blew out the lamp, but instead of rolling over to sleep, she folded her arms beneath her head and stared up into the sky. A fragrant breeze was blowing from the southwest, and overhead a billion stars twinkled in the heavens. She sighed and thought of Phil. *Somewhere, perhaps a thousand miles away, he's probably lying in a sleeping bag near a river, tired from a day of rafting and fun, just like I'm tired from a day of wagon training and fun. Even when we're far away from one another, we're doing exactly the same thing at the same time.* Sighing happily, she started to gaze at one star that had a reddish twinkle and remembered what Carole had said about absence making the heart grow fonder. She pictured Phil's warm smile; then suddenly Gabriel's face flashed before her. She frowned. That wasn't supposed to happen! Suddenly she heard a whisper.

"Stevie? Why are you still awake?"

Stevie turned and looked at Lisa. "I don't know. I just am."

"What are you thinking about?"

"Yeah, Stevie," Carole chimed in. "I could tell you weren't asleep, too." She sat up in her sleeping bag.

Stevie raised herself on one elbow. "Actually, I was thinking about Phil. About how neat it is that he and I are probably a thousand miles apart but we're still doing exactly the same thing. You know, sleeping under the stars and everything."

"That is neat," agreed Lisa.

Then Stevie sighed again and idly snapped a button on her sleeping bag. "But I was also thinking about Gabriel."

"Gabriel?" Lisa asked in disbelief.

Stevie nodded. "You know how annoying he is—how

he puts on that Mr. Superior attitude and struts around here like some movie cowboy."

"Yes?"

"Well, there's something else, too. I mean, have you ever noticed how blue his eyes get when he's being such a jerk? And how when he's acting his worst he grins the most mischievous grin in the world? And have you seen the way he wears his hat?"

"Stevie!" Lisa cried. "You've got a crush on him!"

"Shhh!" Stevie hissed. "Don't talk so loud! The whole camp's going to hear you! And besides, I don't have a crush on him. I just think he's kind of interesting, in a way. Don't you think so?"

"Sure," said Carole. "He's fascinating if you like an obnoxious jerk who thinks he knows everything and doesn't mind telling you about it."

"And if you like someone who assumes you're the dumbest person in the world before you've even said a word," Lisa added.

"Oh, I don't think he's that bad." Stevie turned and vigorously fluffed her pillow.

Lisa shook her head. "Look. If we're sitting here in the middle of the night having a conversation about whether or not Gabriel is cute, then we definitely didn't get enough sleep last night! We're so tired, we're probably not thinking straight, and five-thirty in the morning is going to be here in about five minutes."

"She's right." Carole flopped back down in her sleeping bag. "I'm going to sleep. Stevie, you'll have to figure out Gabriel's cuteness quotient all by yourself."

"Okay, okay," Stevie said as her friends rolled over and went to sleep. She snuggled down in her own sleeping bag and closed her eyes, but her mind spun with thoughts of Phil and Gabriel. *Okay, she told herself, so you find that a basically obnoxious boy has some attractive features. So what? It doesn't mean you have some big-deal crush on him. You just realize that jerks can have nice qualities, too.* She looked over at Carole and Lisa. *You certainly don't have to make excuses to your friends for that. But*—she frowned as she looked at Carole—*didn't Carole say that absence would make my heart grow fonder? If my heart's growing fonder of Phil, then why are my eyes suddenly starting to wander? And what if Phil's eyes are wandering just like mine? What if a thousand miles away there's some cute Ms. Know-It-All on his rafting trip? Or maybe she isn't Ms. Know-It-All. Maybe she's Ms. Cuter-and-Smarter-Than-Me. Maybe she's even a better rider!* Stevie sat up straight in her sleeping bag, her heart thudding. *What if Phil's a thousand miles away falling in love with someone else?*

For a long time she stared at the dim orange glow of the banked campfire, almost wishing she'd canceled this trip and gone rafting with Phil and his family. Then at least if their hearts hadn't grown fonder, their eyes could only have wandered toward each other. Now there was probably some other wonderful, fabulous girl Phil had fallen for. *Oh, well*. She sighed as she once again flopped down in her sleeping bag. There was nothing she could do about Phil and his gorgeous new girlfriend that night. That night the only thing she could do was sleep, and that didn't sound like a half-bad idea.

IT SEEMED AS IF Stevie had just closed her eyes when the clang of the triangle jarred her awake. For a moment she lay in her sleeping bag, watching as Lisa and Carole scurried around getting dressed and brushing their teeth in a small wooden bucket of water.

"Come on, Stevie," Lisa said. "Get up. You're going to be late for breakfast."

Stevie rubbed her eyes. "You two go on over to the chuck wagon and save me a place in the chow line."

"Are you feeling okay?" asked Carole, knowing that Stevie was seldom late for a meal.

Stevie nodded. "I'll catch up to you in a minute."

Lisa and Carole walked over to breakfast while

Stevie rose slowly from her sleeping bag. She climbed into the wagon and found her tattered, scratchy dress. *Phil's new girlfriend probably wears really cool rafting outfits,* she thought glumly, changing from her T-shirt and shorts into the dress. *At least he's not here to see me in this getup.*

After she brushed her hair, she made her way over to the chow line. Lisa and Carole were about to be served. Stevie hurried and slipped in line behind Carole.

"Stevie, why are you such a storm cloud this morning?" Carole asked.

"I didn't sleep too well last night," Stevie muttered as she picked up a tin plate and spoon.

"Look what Mr. Assistant Trail Boss is doing this morning," Lisa whispered with a grin.

Stevie looked up at the steaming iron kettle at the head of the line. Gabriel stood there, helping Shelly spoon cornmeal mush onto everyone's plate.

Maybe I'll skip breakfast, Stevie thought as the line inched forward. Just as she was about to excuse herself, Gabriel saw her and grinned.

"Well, here's the ghost-story queen of Virginia and all her pals," he said as he slapped a serving of mush onto Lisa's plate. "I want to remind you ladies that it's probably not a good day to do any more wagon racing. We're going to be crossing the river, and that can be dangerous."

"No kidding," Stevie said with a smirk.

Gabriel slapped some mush onto her plate. "So you need to be extra careful and pay attention to what the trail bosses tell you to do."

Stevie had opened her mouth to reply when Carole grabbed her arm. "Come on, Stevie. Let's have a nice, peaceful breakfast over there by the tree."

Lisa and Carole hurried Stevie over to a single small pine tree. "You know," Carole said as she sat down beneath the scraggly tree, "I think he must be the biggest jerk I've ever met."

Stevie sat down. Amazingly, she suddenly felt wonderful. As she listened to Carole it occurred to her that she couldn't possibly be interested in someone that painfully obnoxious. She might appreciate some things about him, but like him? Forget it! And that meant that Phil couldn't possibly be interested in the girl he'd just met. Oh, he might like her eyes and her laugh and her cute outfits, but that didn't mean he was going to do anything drastic, like fall in love with her!

Stevie started beaming. "You know," she said to her puzzled friends, "this might turn out to be the best day yet!"

After breakfast Jeremy called a brief camp meeting. "I want to explain a little bit about river crossings," he said, taking off his hat in the bright sunlight. "This river we're crossing today can be dangerous, but we're going over at its widest, shallowest point. We haven't had a lot of rain, so the water should be at a manageable level. For those of you riding horses or tending livestock, the best way to cross is to simply ride or lead your horse or cow into the water. Most animals are natural swimmers and won't have any problem. Don't try to pull them along or make them go any faster than they want to. And of course, if your animal gets into trouble, let it go and get to shore yourself. Animals know how to take care of themselves."

Jeremy looked at Stevie. "For you wagoneers, just drive your team into the river. The horses will swim, and your wagon will float. It also may leak a little, so the trick is to get across as fast as you safely can. That way your supplies won't get too wet. Again, if your wagon should get into trouble, leave it and get to shore yourself."

Jeremy looked at the suddenly grim faces of the campers and smiled. "Let me assure you that I've led wagon trains across this river for fifteen years, and the worst thing I've ever lost was someone's watch." He brushed his gray hair back and resettled his hat. "Okay, pioneers, let's get rolling."

"Are you guys scared?" Carole asked Lisa and Stevie when they were ready to go.

"A little," admitted Stevie. "Although I sure wasn't going to let Jeremy know."

"I just hope Veronica can swim faster than she walks," said Lisa, looking at the placid cow. "Otherwise, she and I might float on down to the Gulf of Mexico."

Suddenly Jeremy's sharp "Wagons ho!" pierced the bright air.

"Good luck, guys," said Stevie, clucking to the horses. "Here we go."

The wagons rolled westward. Slowly the flat land they had been traveling over became hillier, and as they neared the river, gnarled trees climbed up its steep banks. A large flock of yellow-headed blackbirds nested in the trees, cawing in alarm as the wagon train grew near. Stevie maneuvered the wagon as close to the river as she could; then The Saddle Club watched as the wagon ahead of them began to make the crossing.

It crossed the blue water quickly. It floated a little off course in the middle of the stream, but nothing fell off, and the horses pulled it well up on the opposite bank.

"Next!" Jeremy called.

"Our turn," said Stevie. "Why don't you two go first? That other wagon didn't have livestock with it. You guys can get Nikkia and Veronica across, then come back and help me with Yankee and Doodle."

"Good idea," said Carole. She looked at Lisa. "Do you want to go first or shall I?"

"Better let me start," said Lisa. "It'll probably take Veronica three hours to wander across anyway."

"Good luck," Stevie and Carole called as Lisa led Veronica down to the river.

"See you in Acapulco," Lisa laughed.

Lisa stopped on the riverbank. The water, which had looked like a lazy stream from where they had watched the first wagon cross, now seemed more like a rushing torrent. She wondered how deep it was in the middle, then decided it didn't matter. She was on this trip and she was a pioneer. Somehow she would have to get this cow across this river. "Ready, Veronica?" she asked. Veronica looked at the river and continued chewing her cud.

"Well, I'll take that as a big yes," Lisa said. She grasped the lead rope tightly, took a deep breath, and waded into the cold water. She fully expected to feel a tug on the rope, which would mean that Veronica had planted herself firmly on the shore, but to her surprise, Veronica's head began bobbing along right beside her. "Way to go, Veronica!" Lisa said, stunned at the cow's strong, even strokes. "You're a regular mermaid!" Veronica's determined expression looked so comical that Lisa laughed, stepped in a hole, and wound up gulping a mouthful of river water. Suddenly she realized that Veronica was doing fine and she was the one who'd better pay more attention. After a few quick swimming strokes of her own, she pulled Veronica triumphantly to the other side of the river, sending Carole and Stevie a thumbs-up sign.

Next it was Carole's turn. "Come on, Nikkia," Carole said. "Time to go for a swim." The big Appaloosa looked at the water dubiously and backed up a step. Carole urged him forward. He took a sideways step toward the river and stopped. "Let's go, Nikkia," Carole repeated. The horse snorted and shook his head. "Okay. Don't say I didn't warn you," Carole said firmly. She shifted her weight forward in the saddle and gave the horse a loud pop on his rump. Surprised, Nikkia bounded into the river. For a moment Carole thought he might rear, but he found his swimming stride quickly and in a little while they were both shaking water off on the other bank.

"Let's go back and get Stevie now," Lisa said, holding Nikkia's bridle while Carole dismounted from the dripping horse. They tethered Nikkia and Veronica to a nearby tree and then swam back across the river to Stevie.

"Yankee and Doodle seem pretty calm," said Stevie as Lisa and Carole waded out of the river. "I think they've done this before."

"That's a relief," said Carole.

Lisa grabbed Yankee's halter while Carole took hold

of Doodle's, and slowly they led the horses into the river. At first the wagon just creaked along the sandy bottom, but then, as the river deepened, the current lifted and buoyed the wagon. "We're floating!" Stevie called. "We're now officially a boat!"

They reached the other side of the river quickly. The horses shook the water from their coats. Lisa and Carole let go of their halters and Stevie drove them close to where Nikkia and Veronica were tied. "Good boys!" She rubbed them both as she tied them to a tree. "I'm going to sneak you two an apple after lunch!" Suddenly she turned. Someone down by the river was screaming.

She ran back down to the bank. Midway across the river, a wagon had turned over. Though the horses and passengers were safe, all the wagon's supplies were drifting downstream. People on the bank were yelling at Carole and Lisa, who were already swimming out to rescue everything they could grab.

"Wait for me!" cried Stevie, tearing off her boots and hurrying to the shore. She waded into the water and started swimming just as someone else plunged into the river behind her.

Carole and Lisa had spread out in the water. "You grab those bedrolls," Carole called to Lisa. "I'll try to get this backpack."

"What should I get?" asked Stevie, paddling frantically.

"Anything else you can," called Lisa.

A cell phone floated by Stevie's ear. She grabbed it and looked around for something else that might be drifting away, but instead of seeing spilled supplies, she saw Gabriel behind her, grappling with a huge, over-stuffed suitcase.

"Here," she said, swimming over to him. "Let me help."

"Lift one end up and it won't get so wet," he said, spitting out a mouthful of water.

Together they maneuvered the suitcase to the river-bank just as Lisa and Carole waded out with all the bedrolls and the backpack. A crowd of people gathered around as they came ashore.

"Oh, girls," a pretty blond woman said as they stood gasping for breath. "I can't thank you enough! You've saved all our important supplies!"

"And you girls did it just like the real pioneers!" Polly said.

"They didn't save my teddy bear!" shrieked a small voice behind Stevie. She knew without looking whose voice that was. It was little Eileen's.

Mr. Cate started to laugh at Eileen. "Why is a big girl like you crying about a teddy bear? Your parents could have lost everything they brought with them!"

"Because it was *my* teddy bear!" Eileen shrieked even

more loudly. "Mommy! They lost Teddy! They lost *my* Teddy!"

"Shhh, Eileen," said her mother, suddenly embarrassed. She leaned over and wrapped her arms around the weeping girl. "Let's sit over here on the bank with Daddy and calm down."

Suddenly Jeremy rushed up. "Is everyone okay?" he asked.

"Sure," said Gabriel. "We're fine."

"That was quite a rescue you put on. I was busy with their horses, but I saw most of it. The four of you certainly work well together as a team." Jeremy smiled.

"Actually, we did," replied Stevie, glaring at Gabriel. "Imagine that. Menfolk and womenfolk, working together."

Gabriel ignored her and looked at Jeremy, who was squinting at the wagons waiting on the far shore. "After the rest of the wagons cross the river, we'll be on our way," Jeremy said. "We won't go too much farther today, so you folks can take it easy. A river crossing kind of takes the starch out of everybody."

"You can say that again," laughed Lisa, wringing a stream of water out of her skirt.

By midafternoon the wagon train had stopped for the night. Stevie, Carole, and Lisa gave a sigh of relief as the wagons made their traditional circle, a formation the pioneers used to enclose their livestock more than to protect against Indians. As the girls pulled into position, their river-soaked clothes struck to their backs, and Lisa's wet socks squelched with every step she took.

"I vote we dress modern for a little while," she said as Stevie pushed the wagon's brake. "And try to get our pioneer clothes dry somehow."

"Sounds good to me," said Stevie.

They changed into their jeans and hung their wet clothes on some scrub pine that was growing near their wagon. Their normal clothes felt wonderfully comfortable, and for a long time they just relaxed on the ground, letting the afternoon sun warm their stiff muscles as it dried their dresses.

Suddenly Carole frowned. "Do you guys feel anything weird?"

"Weird like how?" Stevie asked.

"I don't know," said Carole. "It's like the ground is tingling."

"Tingling?" Stevie leaned over and put her hand flat on the sandy ground. "Good grief!" she cried. "It *is* tingling! Maybe we're sitting on some kind of underground volcano that's about to blow!"

"Hi, girls," Shelly Bean called, hurrying by. "Are you feeling the cattle yet?"

"The cattle?" Lisa asked.

"Yeah. The herd from the dude ranch. Just put your

hand to the ground and you can feel their hooves."
Shelly grinned and pointed over his shoulder. "You can
also see the dust they're raising on the horizon."

The girls looked where Shelly pointed. Sure enough,
a small cloud of brown dust was slowly drawing closer.

"So much for your underground volcano," Carole
laughed as Stevie's face turned red.

They watched as the dust cloud grew bigger. Finally
they could pick out individual riders moving a mass of
cows toward the river.

"Let's go over and say hello," Carole said, standing
on tiptoe as she watched the herd.

The girls joined some others in their group and
walked over to the dude ranch camp. An array of people much like their own greeted them—families, a couple of teenagers, and a few retired couples. They all
seemed comfortable on their cow ponies and eager to
share tales of their trip with the Oregon Trail folks.

"We hear you guys crossed the river today," a red-
headed young wrangler said.

"That's right," replied Stevie. "Some of us did it
more than once."

"Was it hard getting your wagons across?" a sun-
burned woman asked.

"Probably not as hard as two hundred cows," laughed
Carole.

A little boy in a white cowboy hat rode up on a fat

black pony. "Have you heard that we're going to have a big party tonight?"

"Yes," said Lisa. "And we're really looking forward to it."

"Our trail boss, Robbie, is going to play his fiddle and one of the cowboys is going to call a square dance!"

"That sounds like fun," said Stevie. She turned to Carole and Lisa. "Maybe we'd better go back to our camp and get into our outfits again."

"Good idea," Carole agreed. They said good-bye to their new cowboy friends and hurried back to their camp. Just when they had gotten their pioneer clothes back on, they heard the dinner triangle clanging loudly.

"Come and get it!" Shelly Bean had hopped up on a hay bale and was making a speech. "Tonight my buddy Sidewinder Slim and I have cooked y'all the most delicious, mouthwaterin', lip-smackin', hair-curlin' meal west of the Missouri! And anybody who ain't had two helpings before sundown is gonna hurt my feelings!"

"Whoa!" Carole laughed. "I guess we'd better go eat!"

They joined the others around a huge campfire. Shelly and Sidewinder Slim had truly come up with a feast, filling everybody's plates with thick steaks, piles of corn on the cob, and rhubarb-and-apple cobbler for dessert. Stevie, Lisa, and Carole ate until they couldn't eat anymore.

"Arrgggh," groaned Stevie. "I'm stuffed."

"You can't be stuffed now, Stevie," said Carole. "The dancing is about to begin."

Just as everybody finished supper, a cowboy from the dude ranch stood up by the campfire.

"Howdy, folks. My name's Rascal Robbie Robertson and I'm the head drover for this cattle drive. Tonight I'm going to prove that I can outfiddle anybody east of California and west of Nevada." He struck a chord on his fiddle. "And while I'm sawin' on this thing, my buddy Willowbark Bob here's gonna call some dances for you. So grab a partner and let's have some fun!"

Everybody cleared a large space in front of the fire. Rascal Robbie started to play, and soon six couples were dancing in a square to Willowbark Bob's calls.

A tall boy from the dude ranch came over and asked Lisa to dance, and then Stevie and Carole got up and danced with each other. As they did a ladies' chain around the square, Stevie noticed that Gabriel was dancing with one of the girls from the dude ranch. *Probably too chicken to dance with any of us*, she thought as she and Carole locked arms and swung each other in a wide circle.

Everyone danced until late in the evening. Only Eileen wasn't having fun. She complained to anyone who would listen that Stevie and Carole and Lisa and Gabriel had lost her teddy bear in the river on purpose.

Though everyone was sorry she'd lost her toy, nobody paid much attention to her accusations. Finally she gave up and wandered away by herself.

Later, when the fire had burned to embers, Rascal Robbie said it was time for his cowboys to go put their dogies to sleep, and the party broke up. The cowboys and the pioneers shook hands and wished each other good luck as they walked slowly back to their camps.

"Wasn't that the best time ever?" Lisa said as the girls pulled their sleeping bags out into the open air.

"It was great," said Carole. "And who was that boy you were dancing with? He was cute."

"He said his name was Ken," Lisa replied. "And he was cute, wasn't he? Too bad he's a cowboy and not a pioneer." She nestled down into her sleeping bag. "Are you writing again tonight, Stevie?" she asked.

"Yeah. Just a little." Stevie lit the oil lamp and wrote quickly.

Day Four
What a perfect day! We crossed the river, rescued some cargo, had a campfire and a hoedown. I wish Phil had been here—he would really have enjoyed it.

She read over her words once, blew out the lamp, and shoved the journal under her pillow. She was too tired to write anymore. She could fill in the details later.

Just as she closed her eyes to go to sleep, she heard an ugly howling sound. She lifted her head off the pillow and listened more closely, then shook her head and relaxed again. *Just the wind blowing through the scrub brush. Or maybe it's Gabriel,* she thought with a chuckle as she drifted off to sleep. *Trying to play some trick to prove he's scarier than me.*

CAROLE WOKE UP with a start. She'd been dreaming that
a swarm of bees was chasing her and Starlight. They
were getting closer and closer, and as fast as Starlight
galloped, he couldn't outrun them.

Maybe I shouldn't have eaten so much cobbler, she
thought as she rolled over in her sleeping bag. She
fluffed her pillow and laid her head down. Oddly,
she heard the same buzzing noise she'd just dreamed
about. She lifted her head. The noise was gone. She
laid her head back down. The noise was back.

"That's weird," she said aloud, sitting up. She put the
palm of her hand down on the ground between her

sleeping bag and Stevie's. The buzzing noise became more of a pounding. She felt the ground next to Lisa. It pounded even harder there. She blinked for a moment, and her heart skipped a beat. Suddenly she knew exactly what the noise was. The cattle were stampeding!

In a flash she was out of her sleeping bag. "Stevie! Lisa! Wake up! It's a stampede!"

"Uh?" said Stevie, blinking.

"The cattle are stampeding. And since they're down by the river, the only direction they can run is straight for our camp. We've got to stop them!"

Without another word, the girls scrambled into their jeans and boots. "What shall we do?" asked Lisa.

"We need to get to the corral and get on some horses, and wake up as many people as we can along the way."

"What if everyone panics?" Stevie's eyes were wide with alarm.

"We'll have to let Jeremy worry about that. If they get trampled by a herd of cattle, they'll be dead!"

The girls leaped out of their wagon and raced toward the corral. Carole and Stevie yelled, "Stampede! Everybody up!" while Lisa desperately looked for Jeremy. Most people just blinked at them sleepily, but a few understood what was going on. Karen Nicely wrapped a blanket around her shoulders and ran to warn the next wagon, while Mr. Cate hurried over to Shelly's chuck wagon to ring the triangle. Several cowboys from the dude ranch hurried to put their boots on as well.

The girls ran to the corral, where the dude ranch ponies were mixed in with the wagon train horses. "Shall we just grab anybody?" asked Lisa as the girls threaded their way through the nervous herd.

"Get a cow pony," said Carole. "They'll be easier to mount and they'll know what to do with the cattle."

The girls found three of the ponies in one corner of the corral, their noses pointed toward the cows, as if they sensed what was going on. They calmly allowed Stevie, Carole, and Lisa to hop on their backs, and they did not seem confused by the lack of a saddle and bridle.

"Okay," said Carole. "I'll let you two out of the corral, then we'll ride to the cattle together."

Carole unlatched the makeshift gate and soon all three girls were headed for the runaway herd.

"Hey, wait up!" someone called.

They looked back at the corral. Gabriel was waving at them. He'd hopped on a larger horse, but no one was there to open the gate for him. He looked around once, then dug his heels into the horse's side. The big bay bounded into a gallop and leaped over the corral fence.

"Wow," said Stevie in spite of herself as he galloped up.

"About six ranch hands are right behind me," he

112

called breathlessly. "They said to ride down to the top of the herd and try to head the cattle off from this direction."

"Okay," said Carole. "Let's go!"

Clutching their horses' manes, all four riders galloped into the night. They held on tightly with their legs as the wind whipped their faces. A quarter of a mile away, they could see huge numbers of cattle thundering toward them.

"Rascal Robbie said to fan out and make a lot of noise," Gabriel yelled. "That should confuse them and make them stop."

"Okay," yelled Carole back. She pointed to the left. "You and Stevie go that way. Lisa and I will go over here."

"What sort of noise are we supposed to make?" called Lisa.

"Cowboy noises, I guess." For once Gabriel seemed at a loss. "Something like this." He guided his horse to the left, threw back his head, and shrieked a loud *"Yeeeee-hiiiiiii!"* that echoed against the distant hills.

"Let's go, then!" said Carole.

Stevie veered off and rode along beside Gabriel, screaming like a banshee. Carole and Lisa galloped to the right, doing their own versions of cowboy yells. They rode straight at the oncoming herd. At first the herd kept thundering along, but then the cattle slowed as they became aware of the four screaming riders rushing toward them.

"They're slowing down a little!" called Stevie, yelling over all the hoofbeats. "But they're sure not stopping!"

"Ride closer to me," answered Gabriel. "Maybe we can divide them up and push some of them in another direction."

Stevie moved closer to Gabriel, and together they rode at the left third of the herd. Carole looked over, realized what their strategy was, and did the same thing with Lisa. The two pairs of riders would split the herd into three parts, leaving the middle part for the cowboys to take care of. They all realized it was a long shot, but it was the best chance they had.

"*Yeee-hiiiii!*" shouted Gabriel again, urging his horse to go faster. Stevie did the same thing. So did Lisa and Carole. For a moment the herd kept roaring at them as one huge mass; then a few lead steer on Stevie and Gabriel's side began to turn off. As they turned, all the cattle behind them followed. The herd was dividing!

"Oh, wow!" Stevie yelled, watching as the cattle turned and galloped away from the camp. "It actually worked!"

"Yeah, it did!" whooped Gabriel.

They looked over at Carole and Lisa. The strategy had worked for them, too. The right-hand part of the herd had also turned and was now running east. Stevie could see Carole and Lisa waving at them in triumph. She waved back, but then looked at the smaller part of the herd that was still thundering toward the camp.

"What shall we do about them?" she asked Gabriel.

"I don't think we'll need to worry about them," he said. "Look!"

Stevie looked behind her. Bearing down on the cattle were six cowboys, waving their hats and swinging lassoes. Again the cattle slowed down and then swerved, some following Stevie's herd, others Carole's. Five of the cowboys followed them. The other rode up to Stevie and Gabriel. It was Rascal Robbie.

"I reckon my boys can take care of things now," he said. "These cattle probably won't run much farther."

Carole and Lisa rode up, out of breath. "Is everything okay?" Lisa asked.

"Everything's fine, now," said Rascal Robbie. "I was just about to say your teamwork really saved the day. Those cattle would have mashed flat everything in the camp if it hadn't been for you four. That was some fancy riding you were doing there."

Stevie reached down and gave her pony a pat.

Rascal Robbie tipped his cowboy hat. "Well, I guess I'd better run along and see what's going on. Thanks again. You're mighty brave folks." He turned his horse and rode toward the bulk of the herd. Lisa, Carole, Stevie, and Gabriel sat on their horses and watched as he faded into the night.

"Is everybody okay?" asked Carole.

"We are," said Stevie, glancing at Gabriel. "Although my throat's awfully sore from all that cowboy yelling."

"I feel like I'm covered in dust." Lisa rubbed her eyes.

"Why don't we ride over to the river?" suggested Carole. "We can give the horses a drink and go for a midnight swim."

"You guys go ahead," said Gabriel. "I'm going back to camp to report to Jeremy." He turned his horse and loped off.

"And thanks to you, too, Mr. Assistant Trail Boss," muttered Stevie.

The girls rode over to the river. The tired, sweaty ponies took long swallows of the cool water while the girls took off their jeans and waded into the river, washing away the dirt and dust from the stampeding cattle. They were floating leisurely in the deeper water when Stevie heard a strangely familiar sobbing.

"Hey!" She raised her head. "Listen! That's the same weird sound I heard just before I went to sleep!"

The girls listened. Drifting over the gurgle of the river came an ugly, gasping wail.

Lisa looked around nervously. "What kind of animal makes a noise like that?"

"Look!" said Carole. "Downstream on that rock! It's Eileen!"

The girls looked where Carole pointed. Huddled on a rock overhanging the river sat Eileen, yowling like a wounded cat. "Teddy!" Her heartrending sobs echoed across the water. "Oh, my poor, lost Teddy!"

"Can you believe that?" whispered Lisa. "She's probably been there all night looking for her teddy bear!"

"I can believe it," Stevie replied. "You know what else I can believe? I can believe that awful yowling is what started the stampede in the first place. That little girl and her stupid teddy bear almost got everyone killed!"

Suddenly Eileen's parents appeared. "Eileen!" her father's voice rang out sternly. "Where have you been? Everyone's been searching for you!"

"I've been down here looking for Teddy," Eileen sobbed.

"Well, you climb back up here right now! We thought you'd been killed in the stampede!"

The girls watched as Eileen climbed up the riverbank to rejoin her parents. "Thank goodness they found her," said Lisa. "Otherwise she might have stayed out here yowling and started the stampede all over again."

"Oh, I'm going to take a good swim," said Stevie, "and just wash that little creep out of my system."

With long, smooth strokes, Stevie swam upstream, then flipped over and began floating back to Carole and Lisa. She was lazily dangling her hands and arms in the water when she felt something squishy brush against her fingertips.

"Hey!" she called to her friends. "I just felt something weird. I'm going down to investigate." She dived and ran her hands along the river bottom. Tangled in some underwater branches was the distinct form of a small stuffed animal. Stevie gave the thing a yank and surfaced with it in her hand. She opened her eyes. Sure enough, it was a dripping, dirty teddy bear.

"Hey!" she cried again. "Look what I found!"

"Eileen's teddy bear!" Carole and Lisa said together.

Stevie looked at the mangy thing in disgust. "You know, it would serve her right if I just dropped this back in the river and let it float all the way to the Gulf of Mexico."

"It would," Carole agreed.

Stevie dangled the bear over the water, considering her options. She looked at it for a long moment. Then she threw it back onshore.

"I thought you were going to send Teddy down the river," Lisa said, surprised.

"Oh, I probably should," grumbled Stevie. "But after everything else we've done tonight, it just doesn't seem right."

They climbed out of the river and let themselves air-dry in the grass. When they were only slightly damp, they got up, took the now cool ponies back to their corral, then walked back to camp. "Let's go make our special delivery," said Stevie, turning toward Eileen's wagon. "Then let's go to bed."

The girls knocked on the back of the wagon. Eileen's father stuck his head out around the canvas flap. "Well, hello, girls," he said, sounding surprised to see them. "Can I help you?"

"Well, we were swimming in the river and found this." Stevie held up the bedraggled bear. "I think it must belong to Eileen."

"Oh, my goodness!" cried Eileen's father. "Helen! Come here! Look what these girls have found!"

Eileen's mother stuck her head out of the wagon. "Oh," she cried, tears welling up in her eyes. "Eileen's Teddy! She'll be so thrilled. Let me wake her up right now so she can thank you herself!"

"Oh, no, that's okay," Stevie said, quickly backing away from the wagon. "Eileen doesn't need to thank us.

Let her keep on sleeping. Seeing her sweet smile again tomorrow will be thanks enough!"

"Thank you so much, girls," Eileen's father said as they all backed away. "You don't know what this means to us!"

The girls turned toward their wagon. Most of the campers had gone back to bed, but a few were still up and talking about the events of the night.

"Here come the heroes!" Mr. Cate called as the girls passed by his wagon. "How does it feel to have saved the camp from certain death?"

"Actually, it feels pretty tired, Mr. Cate," Carole yawned.

Karen Nicely laughed. "Haven't you heard? We all get a holiday tomorrow! Jeremy said we can all sleep in as late as we want. And anybody who wakes you three up will have to eat dust at the end of the train for the rest of the trip!"

The girls looked at each other sleepily. "Hey," Stevie said softly, holding her hand up for a high fifteen. "All right!"

They found their camp in the same jumble they'd left it in hours before, when they'd first heard the stampede. Without bothering to straighten anything up, they collapsed into their sleeping bags and fell into a deep and dreamless sleep.

LISA WOKE UP first the next day. A scrub jay squawking
in the brush near their wagon woke her, and when she
opened her eyes she saw that the sun was higher in the
sky than it had been any other morning they'd been on
the trip. She yawned. It felt as if they'd slept forever.
How nice it was of Jeremy to call a holiday after everything that had happened the night before. She wondered if Carole and Stevie had slept as soundly as she
had.

"Anybody else awake?" she asked without lifting her
head from her pillow.

"I am," Carole said through a deep, relaxed yawn.

"I am, too," added Stevie. "Ever since that bird

started singing." She sat up and rubbed her eyes in the morning light. "Gosh. Look how bright it is. It must be close to noon."

"Actually, it's only seven-thirty," said Carole, checking her watch. "It just feels like noon."

"Wasn't it great to sleep in?" Stevie sighed and stretched her arms.

"It was," Carole agreed. "But I think we earned it. We did an awful lot of important stuff yesterday."

"We did, didn't we?" said Lisa. "We got our wagon across the river and we saved Eileen's family's supplies and we stopped a cattle stampede."

"And I returned that dear little brat's precious teddy bear," said Stevie. "We did do a lot yesterday. No wonder I'm starving now." She unzipped her sleeping bag and stood up. "Let's go see if anything's left for breakfast."

They dressed quickly and hurried to the chuck wagon. Instead of the usual pot of steaming mush, the girls found Shelly waiting to cook them a special breakfast of flapjacks and maple syrup.

"Boss's orders." Shelly grinned as he heaped a tall stack of flapjacks on each of their plates. "Today we're celebrating a special occasion, and we're eating high on the hog, just like the pioneers would have."

"Do you know what happened to the rest of the cattle last night?" Stevie asked as Shelly ladled lots of warm maple syrup over her flapjacks.

"That cowboy Rascal Robbie came by here this morning and said they raced for another quarter mile or so, then just ran out of steam. They herded 'em back by the river and gathered up the stragglers this morning, then went on their way." Shelly chuckled. "Rascal Robbie also said to 'thank those three brave girls who helped so much last night.' "

"He thinks we're brave." Lisa looked surprised.

The girls finished their flapjacks by Shelly's campfire and hurried back to their wagon. Even though Jeremy had declared it a holiday, that didn't mean they could goof off the entire day. They still had a lot of ground to cover, and it would take most of the day to do it.

By nine o'clock everyone was ready to go. Jeremy gave a hearty "Wagons ho!" and the train began to roll west. Stevie called her customary "giddyap" to Yankee and Doodle while Lisa began to tug Veronica along behind her. Carole and Nikkia trotted easily beside them.

"You know, it feels like we've being doing this all our lives," Stevie said, watching Yankee and Doodle as they pulled smoothly against their horse collars.

"I know," said Lisa. "These clothes don't feel strange

anymore, and even Veronica seems like an old pal." She turned and smiled at the slow-moving cow lumbering after her.

"And Nikkia's trot honestly feels smooth." Carole laughed. "I guess Starlight will feel like silk when I ride him again."

Just then Karen Nicely rode up on her buckskin mare. "How are our heroines doing today?"

"We feel great, Karen," said Carole. "How are you?"

"Actually, Shelly said I could ask a favor of you. I was wondering if you would be willing to trade a bucket of Veronica's milk for a quarter wheel of some cheddar cheese I've got."

"It's fine with me," Lisa said. She glanced back at the cow. "And I'm sure it's fine with Veronica."

"Great. I'll check back with you when we stop for lunch."

Just as Karen Nicely trotted off, Mr. Cate walked up.

"Hey, Stevie, have you heard about the new restaurant on the moon?" He grinned up at her.

"No, I haven't, Mr. Cate." Stevie raised one eyebrow.

"They say the food's great, but there's no atmosphere!" Mr. Cate threw back his head and gave a deep belly laugh.

"That's a good one, Mr. Cate," she said, chuckling.

"I knew you'd like it!" Still laughing, Mr. Cate walked over toward his wagon.

The train rolled on. The girls noticed that little Eileen was staring dejectedly out the back of her family's wagon several lengths ahead of them. "Her parents must have wised up," said Carole, "and put her in pioneer time-out."

"Good thing," Lisa replied. "Now at least they can have some fun and not worry about what kind of trouble she might be causing."

"I don't know about you guys, but I'm going to need to wash this dress pretty soon." Stevie sniffed her bodice and grimaced. "It's getting pretty ripe."

"Me too," said Lisa. "Let's wash together at the next creek we stop at. Polly Shaver brought one of those old-timey washboards with her and said we could use it anytime."

Stevie laughed. "I bet once we do our laundry with a washboard, doing it in a washing machine at home won't seem nearly so bad."

After they had traveled a few hours, Carole spotted a huge rock that jutted up from the prairie all by itself.

"Look!" She pointed to the single tall crag that broke the flat line of the horizon.

"I bet that's Miller's Rock!" cried Stevie. "I bet that's where we're going to stop for lunch today."

Just as she spoke, Jeremy took off his hat and waved

it at the rock. Slowly the wagons turned and began to roll toward it. They made good time on the dry ground, and by midday they were pulling to a halt just underneath the great boulder.

"Lunch in half an hour," Shelly called as the trekkers parked their wagons.

"Let's go," said Stevie, leaping to the ground. She and Lisa grabbed two buckets and got fresh water, while Carole brought hay for Vernonica and the horses. After Stevie had used one bucket to water the livestock, Lisa used the other to cool Yankee and Doodle down in the hot sun. As they worked, other members of the wagon train tended to their own livestock and helped each other make sure their wagons were ready for the rest of the trip. Just as the girls finished their chores, Shelly rang the triangle for lunch.

"Look at where we're eating today!" Lisa said as they followed everyone to the chuck wagon.

The girls peered over at Miller's Rock Memorial Park, where several pioneers already sat eating their lunch. A hot dog stand and souvenir shop stood at one end of a busy parking lot, surrounded by crowds of tourists. One frantic mother was trying to calm her two crying children, while another man had his entire family posing in front of the Miller's Rock historic marker as he tried to focus his camera.

"Gosh," said Carole as she waited in the chow line for baked beans and corn bread. "Looks like we're back in the middle of the twentieth century."

"It looks so strange, and we've only been gone for four days," said Lisa.

The girls walked to the picnic area and found an empty table next to a family of five who all wore bright orange "Cummings Exterminating—We Won't Bug You" T-shirts. The family stared at the girls as they sat down in their pioneer costumes to eat their simple meal of corn bread and beans.

"Who are they?" they heard one little girl ask her father.

"Oh, I think they're Pennsylvania Dutch," the father whispered.

The Saddle Club looked at each other and giggled.

"We could explain," Lisa suggested.

Stevie glanced over her shoulder at the man, who was splashing ketchup all over a giant order of french fries. "Forget it," she said, shaking her head. "He'd never understand."

They were just beginning to eat when a shadow fell across their table. They looked up. Gabriel stood there, his plate of lunch in his hand.

"Hi," he said, giving one of his lopsided smiles. "Could I sit with you guys?"

"Oh, are you sure the assistant trail boss ought to be seen eating with a bunch of womenfolk?" Stevie cracked.

"Sure, Gabriel, sit down," Carole said, nudging Stevie in the ribs. She knew as well as Stevie that Gabriel was an obnoxious jerk, but he was part of their wagon train family, so that made him *their* obnoxious jerk. And after all, they had been through a lot together.

"Have you girls had a good morning?" he asked politely, taking off his cowboy hat.

"Yes," replied Lisa. "It actually feels like we've done this all our lives."

"Well, I just wanted to make kind of an apology." He brushed his dark hair back. "I think I might have judged you guys too quickly. All three of you really did a terrific job at the stampede last night." He looked at Carole with his fierce blue eyes. "If you hadn't waked everybody up, there might have been a real disaster."

He smiled at Lisa. "And you did more than your share of turning the herd away." He swallowed. "You guys are all darn good horsewomen."

"Thanks," Stevie said loudly, enjoying the blush that suddenly turned his cheeks red.

"Yeah," Carole and Lisa said together. "Thanks."

Gabriel smiled and ate a piece of corn bread. "You know, you're such good riders, it's too bad you won't be able to compete in any of the open events at the rodeo we're going to tomorrow night." He looked at Stevie and grinned. "I'm going to be in the pole racing and the calf roping. But that stuff is really guy stuff. They'll probably have a cow chip tossing contest for girls."

"A cow chip tossing contest?" Stevie felt her face flush with anger.

"Yeah," Gabriel laughed. "You know, where you take a little cow chip and see how far you can toss it. You'd be great at that, Stevie. I bet you've got quite an arm."

Stevie was speechless. Gabriel ate his last bite of lunch and stood up. "Well, I enjoyed eating with you ladies." He tipped his hat. "See you around."

They watched as he strode back to the wagons. Stevie was the first one to break the silence.

"Do you believe him?" she sputtered.

Carole giggled. "I bet he stays up nights studying his be-the-biggest-jerk-you-can-be manual."

"I don't think he studies it," fumed Stevie. "I think he wrote it!"

Suddenly Lisa stood up. "Come on, girls. Let's go back to the wagon train. It looks like Jeremy is making some kind of announcement."

They left the picnic area and hurried over to the chuck wagon, where Jeremy was talking to a group of pioneers.

"We're going to take a little break today, since we've

made it to Miller's Rock. Our next campsite isn't far away, so we'll be staying here until midafternoon. You can spend the next couple of hours resting or relaxing, or you can climb Miller's Rock if you want. It's a moderate to strenuous climb that takes about two hours, round trip. Just make sure you're back here by three, ready to roll."

The girls looked at the rock. They could already hear Gabriel's voice behind them, advising Karen Nicely on the best way to climb in pioneer clothes.

"What do you think?" Stevie asked, squinting at the tall, craggy rock glowing red in the sun.

"We could try it," said Carole. "It would be neat to be able to say we'd done it."

"We could also relax." Lisa frowned at the sharp granite face of the rock. "I mean, we kind of killed ourselves yesterday and last night."

"You're right," said Stevie. "I vote we take our chances on the ground. I mean, something even more exciting could happen down here."

"That's fine with me," said Carole. "For once, why don't we just sit under a shady tree and wait for the next exciting thing to come along?"

THE GIRLS FOUND a shady tree close to their wagon with a good view of Miller's Rock. While they sprawled on the ground watching several pioneers attempting the climb, their animals rested nearby. Veronica dozed in the bright sunshine, and the horses browsed in the thick prairie grass. From a distance, Mr. Cate's version of "The Tennessee Waltz" floated on the air, and a group of pioneer children ran past them in a fast game of capture the flag. Little Eileen was nowhere to be seen.

"You know, this is really nice." Stevie sighed and relaxed against the tree. "Even though I didn't know any of these people four days ago, I feel completely at home."

"I do, too," said Carole, plucking a blade of grass. "I feel that together we could handle most anything."

"It's Miller's Rock." Lisa smiled mysteriously.

"Huh?" Stevie and Carole said together.

"It's Miller's Rock. Remember what Jeremy said? He guaranteed that by the time we reached Miller's Rock we'd be totally different people. Well, here we are. Totally changed at Miller's Rock. And it only took four days."

"Plus a tipped-over wagon and a stampede and a know-it-all assistant trail boss and a little brat who couldn't get over her missing teddy bear," Stevie reminded them.

"And also the departure of Deborah," said Carole.

"That's true. But you know, I think everybody else has changed, too," said Lisa. "I mean, everybody seems more helpful and more interested in seeing that other people are okay."

"You're right," Carole agreed. "I don't even think Gabriel is as bad as he was. He can be nice when he wants to be."

Lisa smiled. "He wasn't nearly as obnoxious at lunch today. And he *does* have gorgeous eyes!"

"Oh, don't be too sure," said Stevie. "Aren't you forgetting the fact that he was taunting us about the rodeo?" She imitated his words. " 'I'm riding in the races. You girls will have to do the cow chip toss.' "

She snorted. "If that's not obnoxious, I don't know what is."

Carole frowned. "Stevie, give him credit. Did you see the jump he took last night? Over the corral fence with no saddle or bridle? He rides awfully well."

"Oh, he just got lucky," Stevie muttered. For some reason the idea of Gabriel's being a good rider made her mad all over again. She couldn't believe that Lisa and Carole didn't think he was obnoxious anymore. If Gabriel wasn't obnoxious, that would mean that Phil's new girlfriend wasn't obnoxious, either. And if she wasn't obnoxious, what was she? Did she even exist? Stevie scratched her head in dismay. There was so much about Phil's trip she didn't know, and she didn't like the idea of not knowing.

"I've got an idea," said Lisa. "Since we've made it to Miller's Rock and become true pioneers, let's drink a toast." She uncapped her leather canteen. "To The Saddle Club. We can accomplish anything when we work together!"

"To The Saddle Club," Stevie added, "which still has more to accomplish. We have to beat the assistant trail boss at his own game. We'll show him a thing or two at the rodeo!"

Carole laughed. "Stevie! You're on the wrong vacation. You should be reenacting the gold rush to California."

"Yeah, Stevie," giggled Lisa. "Or maybe the Pony Express. You could have been the first one there with the most mail."

Stevie grinned. "Well, maybe I am slightly competitive. But isn't winning something you want to win what teamwork is all about?"

"I suppose," laughed Lisa. She held her canteen in the air and repeated, "To The Saddle Club!"

Stevie and Carole clunked their leather canteens against Lisa's. "To tomorrow," added Stevie. "When The Saddle Club will teach the assistant trail boss a thing or two!"

The girls took a sip from their canteens. Just then Shelly's triangle broke the still air. Their minivacation had ended.

"The trail leads westward again," said Carole.

"Right," Stevie said with a grin. "Westward to the sunset, westward to the rodeo, and westward to all points beyond!"

What happens to The Saddle Club next?
Read Bonnie Bryant's exciting new series
and find out.

High school. Driver's licenses. Boyfriends. Jobs.

A lot of new things are happening, but one thing remains the same: Stevie Lake, Lisa Atwood, and Carole Hanson are still best friends. However, even among best friends some things do change, and problems can strain any friendship . . . but these three can handle it. Can't they?

Read an excerpt from Pine Hollow #1:
The Long Ride.

"Do you think we'll get there in time?" Stevie Lake asked, looking around for some reassuring sign that the airport was near.

"Since that plane almost landed on us, I think it's safe to say that we're close," Carole Hanson said.

"Turn right here," said Callie Forester from the backseat.

"And then left up ahead," Carole advised, picking out directions from the signs that flashed past near the airport entrance. "I think Lisa's plane is leaving from that terminal there."

"Which one?"

"The one we just passed," Callie said.

"Oh," said Stevie. She gripped the steering wheel tightly and looked for a way to turn around without causing a major traffic tie-up.

"This would be easier if we were on horseback," said Carole.

"Everything's easier on horseback," Stevie agreed.

"Or if we had a police escort," said Callie.

"Have you done that?" Stevie asked, trying to maneuver the car across three lanes of traffic.

"I have," said Callie. "It's kind of fun, but dangerous.

It makes you think you're almost as important as other people tell you you are."

Stevie rolled her window down and waved wildly at the confused drivers around her. Clearly her waving confused them more, but it worked. All traffic stopped. She crossed the necessary three lanes and pulled onto the service road.

It took another ten minutes to get back to the right and then ten more to find a parking place. Five minutes into the terminal. And then all that was left was to find Lisa.

"Where do you think she is?" Carole asked.

"I know," said Stevie. "Follow me."

"That's what we've been doing all morning," Callie said dryly. "And look how far it's gotten us."

But she followed anyway.

ALEX LAKE REACHED across the table in the airport cafeteria and took Lisa Atwood's hand.

"It's going to be a long summer," he said.

Lisa nodded. Saying good-bye was one of her least favorite activities. She didn't want Alex to know how hard it was, though. That would just make it tougher on him. The two of them had known each other for four years—as long as Lisa had been best friends with Alex's twin sister, Stevie. But they'd only started dating six months earlier. Lisa could hardly believe that. It seemed as if she'd been in love with him forever.

"But it is just for the summer," she said. The words sounded dumb even as they came out of her mouth. The summer *was* long. She wouldn't come back to Virginia until right before school started.

"I wish your dad didn't live so far away, and I wish the summer weren't so long."

"It'll go fast," said Lisa.

"For you, maybe. You'll be in California, surfing or something. I'll just be here, mowing lawns."

"I've never surfed in my life—"

"Until now," said Alex. It was almost a challenge, and Lisa didn't like it.

"I don't want to fight with you," said Lisa.

"I don't want to fight with you, either," he said, relenting. "I'm sorry. It's just that I want things to be different. Not very different. Just a little different."

"Me too," said Lisa. She squeezed his hand. It was a way to keep from saying anything else, because she was afraid that if she tried to speak she might cry, and she hated it when she cried. It made her face red and puffy, but most of all, it told other people how she was feeling. She'd found it useful to keep her feelings to herself these days. Like Alex, she wanted things to be different, but she wanted them to be very different, not just a little. She sighed. That was slightly better than crying.

"I TOLD YOU SO," said Stevie to Callie and Carole.

Stevie had threaded her way through the airport terminal, straight to the cafeteria near the security checkpoint. And there, sitting next to the door, were her twin brother and her best friend.

"Surprise!" the three girls cried, crowding around the table.

"We just couldn't let you be the only one to say goodbye to Lisa," Carole said, sliding into the booth next to Alex.

"We had to be here, too. You understand that, don't you?" Stevie asked Lisa as she sat down next to her.

"And since I was in the car, they brought me along," said Callie, pulling up a chair from a nearby table.

"You guys!" said Lisa, her face lighting up with joy. "I'm so glad you're here. I was afraid I wasn't going to see you for months and months!"

She *was* glad they were there. It wouldn't have felt right if she'd had to leave without seeing them one more time. "I thought you had other things to do."

"We just told you that so we could surprise you. We did surprise you, didn't we?"

"You surprised me," Lisa said, beaming.

"Me too," Alex said dryly. "I'm surprised, too. I really thought I could go for an afternoon, just *one* afternoon of my life, without seeing my twin sister."

Stevie grinned. "Well, there's always tomorrow," she said. "And that's something to look forward to, right?"

"Right," he said, grinning back.

Since she was closest to the outside, Callie went and got sodas for herself, Stevie, and Carole. When she rejoined the group, they were talking about everything in the world except the fact that Lisa was going to be gone for the summer and how much they were all going to miss one another.

She passed the drinks around and sat quietly at the end of the table. There wasn't much for her to say. She didn't really feel as if she belonged there. She wasn't anybody's best friend. It wasn't as if they minded her being there, but she'd come along because Stevie had offered to drive her to a tack shop after they left the airport. She was simply along for the ride.

". . . And don't forget to say hello to Skye."

"Skye? Skye who?" asked Alex.

"Don't pay any attention to him," Lisa said. "He's just jealous."

"You mean because Skye is a movie star?"

"And say hi to your father and the new baby. It must be exciting that you'll meet your sister."

"Well, of course, you've already met her, but now she's crawling, right? It's a whole different thing."

An announcement over the PA system brought their chatter to a sudden halt.

"It's my flight," Lisa said slowly. "They're starting to board and I've got to get through security and then to Gate . . . whatever."

"Fourteen," Alex said. "It comes after Gate Twelve. There are no thirteens in airports."

"Let's go."

"Here, I'll carry that."

"And I'll get this one. . . ."

As Callie watched, Lisa hugged Carole and Stevie. Then she kissed Alex. Then she hugged her friends again. Then she turned to Alex.

"I think it's time for us to go," Carole said tactfully.

"Write or call every day," Stevie said.

"It's a promise," said Lisa. "Thanks for coming to the airport. You, too, Callie."

Callie smiled and gave Lisa a quick hug before all the girls backed off from Lisa and Alex.

Lisa waved. Her friends waved and turned to leave her alone with Alex. They were all going to miss her, but the girls had one another. Alex only had his lawns to mow. He needed the last minutes with Lisa.

"See you at home!" Stevie called over her shoulder, but she didn't think Alex heard. His attention was completely focused on one person.

Carole wiped a tear from her eye once they'd rounded a corner. "I'm going to miss her."

"Me too," said Stevie.

Carole turned to Callie. "It must be hard for you to understand," she said.

"Not really," said Callie. "I can tell you three are really close."

"We are," Carole said. "Best friends for a long time. We're practically inseparable." Even to her the words sounded exclusive and uninviting. If Callie noticed, she didn't say anything.

The three girls walked out of the terminal and found

their way to Stevie's car. As she turned on the engine, Stevie was aware of an uncomfortable empty feeling. She really didn't like the idea of Lisa's being gone for the summer, and her own unhappiness was not going to be helped by a brother who was going to spend the entire time moping about his missing girlfriend. There had to be something that would make her feel better.

"Say, Carole, do you want to come along with us to the tack shop?" she asked.

"No, I can't," Carole said. "I promised I'd bring in the horses from the paddock before dark, so you can just drop me off at Pine Hollow. Anyway, aren't you due at work in an hour?"

Stevie glanced at her watch. Carole was right. Everything was taking longer than it was supposed to this afternoon.

"Don't worry," Callie said quickly. "We can go to the tack shop another time."

"You don't mind?" Stevie asked.

"No. I don't. Really," said Callie. "I don't want you to be late for work—either of you. If my parents decide to get a pizza for dinner again, I'm going to want it to arrive on time!"

Stevie laughed, but not because she thought anything was very funny. She wasn't about to forget the last time she'd delivered a pizza to Callie's family. In fact, she wished it hadn't happened, but it had. Now she had to find a way to face up to it.

As she pulled out of the airport parking lot, a plane

roared overhead, rising into the brooding sky. *Maybe that's Lisa's plane,* she thought. The noise of its flight seemed to mark the beginning of a long summer.

The first splats of rain hit the windshield as Stevie paid their way out of the parking lot. By the time they were on the highway, it was raining hard. The sky had darkened to a steely gray. Streaks of lightning brightened it, only to be followed by thunder that made the girls jump.

The storm had come out of nowhere. Stevie flicked on the windshield wipers and hoped it would go right back to nowhere.

The sky turned almost black as the storm strengthened. Curtains of rain ripped across the windshield, pounding on the hood and roof of the car. The wipers flicked uselessly at the torrent.

"I hope Fez is okay," said Callie. "He hates thunder, you know."

"I'm not surprised," said Carole, trying to control her voice. It seemed to her that there were a lot of things Fez hated. He was as temperamental as any horse she had ever ridden.

Fez was one of the horses in the paddock. Carole didn't want to upset Callie by telling her that. If she told Callie he'd been turned out, Callie would wonder why he hadn't just been exercised. If she told Callie she'd exercised him, Callie might wonder if he was being overworked. Carole shook her head. What was it about this girl that made Carole so certain that whatever she said, it would be wrong? Why couldn't she say the one thing she really needed to say?

Still, Carole worked at Pine Hollow, and that meant taking care of the horses that were boarding there—and that meant keeping the owners happy.

"I'm sure Fez will be fine. Ben and Max will look after him," Carole said.

"I guess you're right," said Callie. "I know he can be difficult. Of course, you've ridden him, so you know that, too. I mean, that's obvious. But it's spirit, you see. Spirit is the key to an endurance specialist. He's got it, and I think he's got the makings of a champion. We'll work together this summer, and come fall . . . well, you'll see."

Spirit—yes, it was important in a horse. Carole knew that. She just wished she understood why it was that Fez's spirit was so irritating to her. She'd always thought of herself as someone who'd never met a horse she didn't like. Maybe it was the horse's owner. . . .

"Uh-oh," said Stevie, putting her foot gently on the brake. "I think I got it going a little too fast there."

"You've got to watch out for that," Callie said. "My father says the police practically lie in wait for teenage drivers. They love to give us tickets. Well, they certainly had fun with me."

"You got a ticket?" Stevie asked.

"No, I just got a warning, but it was almost worse than a ticket. I was going four miles over the speed limit in our hometown. The policeman stopped me, and when he saw who I was, he just gave me a warning. Dad was furious—at me and at the officer, though he didn't say anything to the officer. He was angry at him because he thought someone would find out and say I'd gotten special treatment! I was only going four miles over the speed limit. Really. Even the officer said that. Well, it would have been easier if I'd gotten a ticket. Instead, I got grounded. Dad won't let me drive for three months. Of course, that's nothing compared to what happened to Scott last year."

"What happened to Scott?" Carole asked, suddenly curious about the driving challenges of the Forester children.

"Well, it's kind of a long story," said Callie. "But—"

"Wow! Look at that!" Stevie interrupted. There was an amazing streak of lightning over the road ahead. The dark afternoon brightened for a minute. Thunder followed instantly.

"Maybe we should pull off the road or something?" Carole suggested.

"I don't think so," said Stevie. She squinted through the windshield. "It's not going to last long. It never does when it rains this hard. We get off at the next exit anyway."

She slowed down some more and turned the wipers up a notch. She followed the car in front of her, keeping a constant eye on the two red spots of the car's taillights. She'd be okay as long as she could see them. The rain pelted the car so loudly that it was hard to talk. Stevie drove on cautiously.

Then, as suddenly as it had started, the rain stopped. Stevie spotted the sign for their exit, signaled, and pulled off to the right and up the ramp. She took a left onto the overpass and followed the road toward Willow Creek.

The sky was as dark as it had been, and there were clues that there had been some rain there, but nothing nearly as hard as the rain they'd left on the interstate. Stevie sighed with relief and switched the windshield wipers to a slower rate.

"I think I'll drop you off at Pine Hollow first," she said, turning onto the road that bordered the stable's property.

Pine Hollow's white fences followed the contour of the road, breaking the open, grassy hillside into a sequence of paddocks and fields. A few horses stood in the fields, swishing their tails. One bucked playfully and ran up a hill, shaking his head to free his mane in the wind. Stevie smiled. Horses always seemed to her the most welcoming sight in the world.

"Then I'll take Callie home," Stevie continued, "and after that I'll go over to Pizza Manor. I may be a few minutes late for work, but who orders pizza at five o'clock in the afternoon anyway?"

"Now, now," teased Carole. "Is that any way for you to mind your Pizza Manors?"

"Well, at least I have my hat with me," said Stevie. Or did she? She looked into the rearview mirror to see if she could spot it, and when that didn't do any good, she glanced over her shoulder. Callie picked it up and started to hand it to her.

"Here," she said. "We wouldn't want— Wow! I guess the storm isn't over yet!"

The sky had suddenly filled with a brilliant streak of lightning, jagged and pulsating, accompanied by an explosion of thunder.

It startled Stevie. She shrieked and turned her face back to the road. The light was so sudden and so bright that it blinded her for a second. The car swerved. Stevie braked. She clutched at the steering wheel and then realized she couldn't see because the rain was pelting even harder than before. She reached for the wiper control, switching it to its fastest speed.

There was something to her right! She saw something move, but she didn't know what it was.

"Stevie!" Carole cried.

"Look out!" Callie screamed from the backseat.

Stevie swerved to the left on the narrow road, hoping it would be enough. Her answer was a sickening jolt as the car slammed into something solid. The car spun around, smashing against the thing again. When the thing screamed, Stevie knew it was a horse. Then it disappeared from her field of vision. Once again, the car spun. It smashed against the guardrail on the left side of the road and tumbled up and over it as if the rail had never been there.

Down they went, rolling, spinning. Stevie could hear

the screams of her friends. She could hear her own voice, echoing in the close confines of the car, answered by the thumps of the car rolling down the hillside into a gully. Suddenly the thumping stopped. The screams were stilled. The engine cut off. The wheels stopped spinning. And all Stevie could hear was the idle *slap, slap, slap* of her windshield wipers.

"Carole?" she whispered. "Are you okay?"

"I think so. What about you?" Carole answered.

"Me too. Callie? Are you okay?" Stevie asked.

There was no answer.

"Callie?" Carole echoed.

The only response was the girl's shallow breathing. How could this have happened?

ABOUT THE AUTHOR

Bonnie Bryant is the author of nearly a hundred books about horses, including The Saddle Club series, Saddle Club Super Editions, and the Pony Tails series. She has also written novels and movie novelizations under her married name, B. B. Hiller.

Ms. Bryant began writing The Saddle Club in 1986. Although she had done some riding before that, she intensified her studies then and found herself learning right along with her characters Stevie, Carole, and Lisa. She claims that they are all much better riders than she is.

Ms. Bryant was born and raised in New York City. She still lives there, in Greenwich Village, with her two sons.

Don't miss the thrilling conclusion to this exciting
Saddle Club adventure . . .

QUARTER HORSE
Saddle Club #82

The Saddle Club is nearing the end of their Oregon
Trail ride. It's been a long journey, and it's about to
get longer: Stevie Lake's competitive personality is
taking over. When a boy on the trip boasts that he
can outdo any mere girl at any kind of horsemanship,
Stevie decides to take up his challenge. Before her
friends know what's happened, Stevie is entering a
rodeo out West.

Has Stevie finally met her match? Can her friends
stop this Wild West duel before things get out of
hand? Or does the young cowboy have something else
in mind when he challenges Stevie to a roping and
hog-tying contest?

PINE HOLLOW

New Series from Bonnie Bryant

Friends always come first ... don't they?

A lot of new things are happening, but one thing remains the same: Stevie, Lisa, and Carole are still best friends.

Even so, growing up and taking on new responsibilities can be difficult. Now with **high school**, **driver's licenses**, **boyfriends**, and **jobs**, they hardly have time for themselves—not to mention each other and their horses!

Then an accident leaves a girl's life in the balance, and someone has to take the blame. Can even best friends survive this test?

Coming July 1998 from Bantam Books.

BFYR 171